The Blind Mother and The Last Confession

The Blind Mother and The Last Confession

Hall Caine

MINT EDITIONS

The Blind Mother and The Last Confession was first published in 1892.

This edition published by Mint Editions 2020.

ISBN 9781513267623 | E-ISBN 9781513272627

Published by Mint Editions®

 MINT
EDITIONS

minteditionbooks.com

Publishing Director: Jennifer Newens
Design & Production: Rachel Lopez Metzger
Typesetting: Westchester Publishing Services

Contents

THE BLIND MOTHER

I

The Vale of Newlands lay green in the morning sunlight; the river that ran through its lowest bed sparkled with purple and amber; the leaves prattled low in the light breeze that soughed through the rushes and the long grass; the hills rose sheer and white to the smooth blue lake of the sky, where only one fleecy cloud floated languidly across from peak to peak. Out of unseen places came the bleating of sheep and the rumble of distant cataracts, and above the dull thud of tumbling waters far away was the thin caroling of birds overhead.

But the air was alive with yet sweeter sounds. On the breast of the fell that lies over against Cat Bell a procession of children walked, and sang, and chattered, and laughed. It was St. Peter's Day, and they were rush-bearing; little ones of all ages, from the comely girl of fourteen, just ripening into maidenhood, who walked last, to the sweet boy of four in the pinafore braided with epaulets, who strode along gallantly in front. Most of the little hands carried rushes, but some were filled with ferns, and mosses, and flowers. They had assembled at the schoolhouse, and now, on their way to the church, they were making the circuit of the dale.

They passed over the road that crosses the river at the head of Newlands, and turned down into the path that follows the bed of the valley. At that angle there stands a little group of cottages deliciously cool in their whitewash, nestling together under the heavy purple crag from which the waters of a ghyll fall into a deep basin that reaches to their walls. The last of the group is a cottage with its end to the road, and its open porch facing a garden shaped like a wedge. As the children passed this house an old man, gray and thin and much bent, stood by the gate, leaning on a staff. A collie, with the sheep's dog wooden bar suspended from its shaggy neck, lay at his feet. The hum of voices brought a young woman into the porch. She was bareheaded and wore a light print gown. Her face was pale and marked with lines. She walked cautiously, stretching one hand before her with an uncertain motion, and grasping a trailing tendril of honeysuckle that swept downward from the roof. Her eyes, which were partly inclined upward and partly turned toward the procession, had a vague light in their bleached pupils. She was blind. At her side, and tugging at her other hand, was a child of a year and a half—a chubby, sunny little fellow with ruddy cheeks, blue eyes, and fair curly hair. Prattling, laughing, singing snatches, and waving their rushes and ferns above their happy, thoughtless heads, the children rattled past. When they were gone the air was empty, as it is when the lark stops in its song.

After the procession of children had passed the little cottage at the angle of the roads, the old man who leaned on his staff at the gate turned about and stepped to the porch.

"Did the boy see them?—did he see the children?" said the young woman who held the child by the hand.

"I mak' na doot," said the old man.

He stooped to the little one and held out one long withered finger. The soft baby hand closed on it instantly.

"Did he laugh? I thought he laughed," said the young woman.

A bright smile played on her lips.

"Maybe so, lass."

"Ralphie has never seen the children before, father. Didn't he look frightened—just a little bit frightened—at first, you know? I thought he crept behind my gown."

"Maybe, maybe."

The little one had dropped the hand of his young mother, and, still holding the bony finger of his grandfather, he toddled beside him into the house.

Very cool and sweet was the kitchen, with white-washed walls and hard earthen floor. A table and a settle stood by the window, and a dresser that was an armory of bright pewter dishes, trenchers, and piggins, crossed the opposite wall.

"Nay, but sista here, laal lad," said the old man, and he dived into a great pocket at his side.

"Have you brought it? Is it the kitten? Oh, dear, let the boy see it!"

A kitten came out of the old man's pocket, and was set down on the rug at the hearth. The timid creature sat dazed, then raised itself on its hind legs and mewed.

"Where's Ralphie? Is he watching it, father? What is he doing?"

The little one had dropped on hands and knees before the kitten, and was gazing up into its face.

The mother leaned over him with a face that would have beamed with sunshine if the sun of sight had not been missing.

"Is he looking? Doesn't he want to coddle it?"

The little chap had pushed his nose close to the nose of the kitten, and was prattling to it in various inarticulate noises.

"Boo—loo—lal-la—mama."

"Isn't he a darling, father?"

"It's a winsome wee thing," said the old man, still standing, with drooping head, over the group on the hearth.

The mother's face saddened, and she turned away. Then from the opposite side of the kitchen, where she was making pretense to take plates from a plate-rack, there came the sound of suppressed weeping. The old man's eyes followed her.

"Nay, lass; let's have a sup of broth," he said, in a tone that carried another message.

The young woman put plates and a bowl of broth on the table.

"To think that I can never see my own child, and everybody else can see him!" she said, and then there was another bout of tears.

The charcoal-burner supped at his broth in silence. A glistening bead rolled slowly down his wizened cheek: and the interview on the hearth went on without interruption:

"Mew—mew—mew. Boo—loo—lal-la—mama."

The child made efforts to drag himself to his feet by laying hold of the old man's trousers.

"Nay, laddie," said the old man, "mind my claes—they'll dirty thy bran-new brat for thee."

"Is he growing, father?" said the girl.

"Growing?—amain."

"And his eyes—are they changing color?—going brown? Children's eyes do, you know."

"Maybe—I'll not be for saying nay."

"Is he—is he *very* like me, father?"

"Nay—well—nay—I's fancying I see summat of the stranger in the laal chap at whiles."

The young mother turned her head aside.

THE OLD MAN'S NAME WAS Matthew Fisher; but the folks of the countryside called him Laird Fisher. This dubious dignity came of the circumstance that he had been the holder of an absolute royalty in a few acres of land under Hindscarth. The royalty had been many generations in his family. His grandfather had set store by it. When the Lord of the Manor had worked the copper pits at the foot of the Eal Crags, he had tried to possess himself of the royalties of the Fishers. But the present families resisted the aristocrat. Luke Fisher believed there was a fortune under his feet, and he meant to try his luck on his holding some day. That day never came. His son, Mark Fisher, carried on the tradition, but made no effort to unearth the fortune. They were a cool, silent, slow, and stubborn race. Matthew Fisher followed his father and his grandfather, and inherited the family pride. All these years the tenders of the Lord of the Manor were ignored, and the Fishers enjoyed their title of courtesy or badinage. Matthew married, and had one daughter called Mercy. He farmed his few acres with poor results. The ground was good enough, but Matthew was living under the shadow of the family tradition. One day—it was Sunday morning, and the sun shone brightly—he was rambling by the Po Bett that rises on Hindscarth, and passed through his land, when his eyes glanced over a glittering stone that lay among the pebbles at the bottom of the stream. It was ore, good full ore, and on the very surface. Then the Laird sank a shaft, and all his earnings with it, in an attempt to procure iron or copper. The dalespeople derided him, but he held silently on his way.

"How dusta find the cobbles to-day—any softer?" they would say in passing.

"As soft as the hearts of most folk," he would answer; and then add in a murmur, "and maybe a vast harder nor their heads."

The undeceiving came at length, and then the Laird Fisher was old and poor. His wife died broken-hearted. After that the Laird never rallied. The shaft was left unworked, and the holding lay fallow. Laird Fisher took wage from the Lord of the Manor to burn charcoal in the wood. The breezy irony of the dalesfolk did not spare the old man's bent head. There was a rime current in the vale which ran:

> *"There's t'auld laird, and t'young laird, and t'laird among t'barns,*
> *If iver there comes another laird, we'll hang him up by t'arms."*

A second man came to Matthew's abandoned workings. He put money into it and skill and knowledge, struck a vein, and began to realize a fortune. The only thing he did for the old Laird was to make him his banksman at a pound a week—the only thing save one thing, and that is the beginning of this story.

The man's name was Hugh Ritson. He was the second son of a Cumbrian statesman in a neighboring valley, was seven-and-twenty, and had been brought up as a mining engineer, first at Cleaton Moor and afterward at the College in Jerman Street. When he returned to

Cumberland and bought the old Laird's holding he saw something of the old Laird's daughter. He remembered Mercy as a pretty prattling thing of ten or eleven. She was now a girl of eighteen, with a simple face, a timid manner, and an air that was neither that of a woman nor of a child. Her mother was lately dead, her father spent most of his days on the fell (some of his nights also when the charcoal was burning), and she was much alone. Hugh Ritson liked her sweet face, her gentle replies, and her few simple questions. It is unnecessary to go further. The girl gave herself up to him with her whole heart and soul. Then he married another woman.

The wife was the daughter of the Vicar, Parson Christian. Her name was Greta: she was beautiful to look upon—a girl of spirit and character. Greta knew nothing of Hugh Ritson's intercourse with Mercy until after he had become her husband. Mercy was then in the depth of her trouble, and Greta had gone to comfort her. Down to that hour, though idle tongues had wagged, no one had lighted on Mercy's lover, and not even in her fear had she confessed. Greta told her that it was brave and beautiful to shield her friend, but he was unworthy of her friendship or he would stand by her side—who was he? It was a trying moment. Greta urged and pleaded and coaxed, and Mercy trembled and stammered and was silent. The truth came out at last, and from that moment the love between the two women was like the love of David and Jonathan. Hugh Ritson was compelled to stand apart and witness it. He could not recognize it; he dared not oppose it; he could only drop his head and hold his tongue. It was coals of fire on his head from both sides. The women never afterward mentioned him to each other, and yet somehow—by some paradox of love—he was the bond between them.

A month before the birth of the child, Mercy became blind. This happened suddenly and without much warning. A little cold in the eyes, a little redness around them and a total eclipse of sight. If such a disaster had befallen a married wife, looking forward to a happy motherhood, death itself might have seemed a doom more kind. But Mercy took it with a sombre quietness. She was even heard to say that it was just as well. These startling words, repeated to Greta, just told her something of the mystery and misery of Mercy's state. But their full meaning, the whole depth of the shame they came from, were only revealed on the morning after the night on which Mercy's child was born.

They were in the room upstairs, where Mercy herself had been born less than nineteen years before: a little chamber with the low eaves and the open roof rising to the ridge: a peaceful place with its white-washed walls and the odor of clean linen. On the pillow of the bed lay the simple face of the girl-mother, with its fair hair hanging loose and its blind eyes closed. Mercy had just awakened from the first deep sleep that comes after all is over, and the long fingers of one of her thin hands were plucking at the white counterpane. In a nervous voice she began to speak. Where was Mrs. Ritson? Greta answered that she was there, and the baby was sleeping on her knee. Anybody else? No, nobody else. Was it morning? Yes, it was eight in the morning, and her father, who had not been to bed, had eaten his breakfast, and lighted his pipe and gone to work. Was the day fine? Very fine. And the sun shining? Yes, shining beautifully. Was the blind down? Yes, the little white blind was down. Then all the room was full of that soft light? Oh, yes, full of it. Except in the corner by the washstand? Well, except in the corner. Was the washstand still there? Why, yes, it was still there. And mother's picture on the wall above it? Oh, dear, yes. And the chest of drawers near the door with the bits of sparkling lead ore on top? Of course. And the texts pinned on to the wall-paper: "Come unto Me"—eh? Yes, they were all there. Then everything was just the same? Oh, yes, everything the same.

"The same," cried Mercy, "everything the same, but, O Lord Jesus, how different!"

The child was awakened by the shrill sound of her voice, and it began to whimper, and Greta to hush it, swaying it on her knee, and calling it by a score of pretty names. Mercy raised her head a moment and listened, then fell back to the pillow and said, "How glad I am I'm blind!"

"Good gracious, Mercy, what are you saying?" said Greta.

"I'm glad I can't see it."

"Mercy!"

"Ah, you're different, Mrs. Ritson. I was thinking of that last night. When your time comes perhaps you'll be afraid you'll die, but you'll never be afraid you'll not. And you'll say to yourself, 'It will be over soon, and then what joy!' That wasn't my case. When I was at the worst I could only think, 'It's dreadful now, but oh, to-morrow all the world will be different.'"

One poor little day changed all this. Toward sunset the child had to be given the breast for the first time. Ah! that mystery of life, that mystery of motherhood, what are the accidents of social law, the big conventions of virtue and vice, of honor and disgrace, before the touch of the spreading fingers of a babe as they fasten on the mother's breast! Mercy thought no more of her shame.

She had her baby for it, at all events. The world was not utterly desolate. After all, God was very good!

Then came a great longing for sight. She only wished to see her child. That was all. Wasn't it hard that a mother had never seen her own baby? In her darkness she would feel its little nose as it lay asleep beside her, and let her hand play around its mouth and over its eyes and about its ears. Her touch passed over the little one like a look. It was almost as if there were sight in the tips of her fingers.

The child lived to be six months old, and still Mercy had not seen him; a year, and yet she had no hope. Then Greta, in pity of the yearning gaze of the blind girl-face whenever she came and kissed the boy and said how bonny he was, sent to Liverpool for a doctor, that at least they might know for a certainty if Mercy's sight was gone forever. The doctor came. Yes, there was hope. The mischief was cataract on both eyes. Sight might return, but an operation would be necessary. That could not, however, be performed immediately. He would come again in a month, and a colleague with him, and meantime the eyes must be bathed constantly in a liquid which they would send for the purpose.

At first Mercy was beside herself with delight. She plucked up the boy and kissed and kissed him. The whole day long she sang all over the house like a liberated bird. Her face, though it was blind, was like sunshine, for the joyous mouth smiled like eyes. Then suddenly there came a change. She plucked up the boy and kissed him still, but she did not sing and she did not smile. A heavy thought had come to her. Ah! if she should die under the doctor's hands! Was it not better to live in blindness and keep her boy than to try to see him and so lose him altogether? Thus it was with her on St. Peter's Day, when the children of the dale went by at their rush-bearing.

THERE WAS THE FAINT SOUND of a footstep outside.

"Hark!" said Mercy, half rising from the sconce. "It's Mrs. Ritson's foot."

The man listened. "Nay, lass, there's no foot," said Matthew.

"Yes, she's on the road," said Mercy. Her face showed that pathetic tension of the other senses which is peculiar to the blind. A moment later Greta stepped into the cottage, with a letter in her hand. "Good-morning, Matthew; I have news for you, Mercy. The doctors are coming to-day."

Mercy's face fell perceptibly. The old man's head dropped lower.

"There, don't be afraid," said Greta, touching her hand caressingly. "It will soon be over. The doctors didn't hurt you before, did they?"

"No, but this time it will be the operation," said Mercy. There was a tremor in her voice.

Greta had lifted the child from the sconce. The little fellow cooed close to her ear; and babbled his inarticulate nothings.

"Only think, when it's all over you will be able to see your darling Ralphie for the first time!"

Mercy's sightless face brightened. "Oh, yes," she said, "and watch him play, and see him spin his tops and chase the butterflies. Oh, that will be very good!"

"Dusta say to-day, Mistress Ritson?" asked Matthew, the big drops standing in his eyes.

"Yes, Matthew; I will stay to see it over, and mind baby, and help a little."

Mercy took the little one from Greta's arms and cried over it, and laughed over it, and then cried and laughed again. "Mama and Ralphie shall play together in the garden, darling; and Ralphie shall see the horses—and the flowers—and the birdies—and mama—yes, mama shall see Ralphie."

II

Two hours later the doctors arrived. They looked at Mercy's eyes, and were satisfied that the time was ripe for the operation. At the sound of their voices, Mercy trembled and turned livid. By a maternal instinct she picked up the child, who was toddling about the floor, and clasped it to her bosom. The little one opened wide his blue eyes at sight of the strangers, and the prattling tongue became quiet.

"Take her to her room, and let her lie on the bed," said one of the doctors to Greta.

A sudden terror seized the young mother. "No, no, no!" she said, in an indescribable accent, and the child cried a little from the pressure to her breast.

"Come, Mercy, dear, be brave for your boy's sake," said Greta.

"Listen to me," said the doctor, quietly but firmly: "You are now quite blind, and you have been in total darkness for a year and a half. We may be able to restore your sight by giving you a few minutes' pain. Will you not bear it?"

Mercy sobbed, and kissed the child passionately.

"Just think, it is quite certain that without an operation you will never regain your sight," continued the doctor. "You have nothing to lose, and everything to gain. Are you satisfied? Come, go away to your room quietly."

"Oh, oh, oh!" sobbed Mercy.

"Just imagine, only a few minutes' pain, and even of that you will scarcely be conscious. Before you know what is doing it will be done."

Mercy clung closer to her child, and kissed it again and yet more fervently.

The doctors turned to each other. "Strange vanity!" muttered the one who had not spoken before. "Her eyes are useless, and yet she is afraid she may lose them."

Mercy's quick ears caught the whispered words. "It is not that," she said, passionately.

"No, gentlemen," said Greta, "you have mistaken her thought. Tell her she runs no danger of her life."

The doctors smiled and laughed a little. "Oh, that's it, eh? Well, we can tell her that with certainty."

Then there was another interchange of half-amused glances.

"Ah, we that be men, sirs, don't know the depth and tenderness of a mother's heart," said old Matthew. And Mercy turned toward him a face that was full of gratitude. Greta took the child out of her arms and hushed it to sleep in another room. Then she brought it back and put it in its cradle that stood in the ingle.

"Come, Mercy," she said, "for the sake of your boy." And Mercy permitted herself to be led from the kitchen.

"So there will be no danger," she said. "I shall not leave my boy. Who said that? The doctor? Oh, good gracious, it's nothing. Only think, I shall live to see him grow to be a great lad."

Her whole face was now radiant.

"It will be nothing. Oh, no, it will be nothing. How silly it was to think that he would live on, and grow up, and be a man, and I lie cold in the churchyard—and me his mother! That was very childish, wasn't it? But, then, I have been so childish since Ralphie came."

"There, lie and be quiet, and it will soon be over," said Greta.

"Let me kiss him first. Do let me kiss him! Only once. You know it's a great risk after all. And if he grew up—and I wasn't here—if—if—"

"There, dear Mercy, you must not cry again. It inflames your eyes, and that can't be good for the doctors."

"No, no, I won't cry. You are very good; everybody is very good. Only let me kiss my little Ralphie—just for the last."

Greta led her back to the side of the cot, and she spread herself over it with outstretched arms, as the mother-bird poises with outstretched wings over her brood. Then she rose, and her face was peaceful and resigned.

The Laird Fisher sat down before the kitchen fire, with one arm on the cradle head. Parson Christian stood beside him. The old charcoal-burner wept in silence, and the good Parson's voice was too thick for the words of comfort that rose to his lips.

The doctors followed into the bedroom. Mercy was lying tranquilly on her bed. Her countenance was without expression. She was busy with her own thoughts. Greta stood by the bedside; anxiety was written in every line of her beautiful, brave face.

"We must give her the gas," said one of the doctors, addressing the other.

Mercy's features twitched.

"Who said that?" she asked nervously.

"My child, you must be quiet," said the doctor in a tone of authority.

"Yes, I will be quiet, very quiet; only don't make me unconscious," she said. "Never mind me; I will not cry. No; if you hurt me I will not cry out. I will not stir. I will do everything you ask. And you shall say how quiet I have been. Only don't let me be insensible."

The doctors consulted together aside, and in whispers.

"Who spoke about the gas? It wasn't you, Mrs. Ritson, was it?"

"You must do as the doctors wish, dear," said Greta in a caressing voice.

"Oh, I will be very good. I will do every little thing. Yes, and I will be so brave. I am a little childish sometimes, but I *can* be brave, can't I?"

The doctors returned to the bedside.

"Very well, we will not use the gas," said one. "You are a brave little woman, after all. There, be still—very still."

One of the doctors was tearing linen into strips for bandages, while the other fixed Mercy's head to suit the light.

There was a faint sound from the kitchen. "Wait," said Mercy. "That is father—he's crying. Tell him not to cry. Say it's nothing."

She laughed a weak little laugh.

"There, he will hear that; go and say it was I who laughed."

Greta left the room on tiptoe. Old Matthew was still sitting over a dying fire, gently rocking the sleeping child.

When Greta returned to the bedroom, Mercy called her, and said, very softly, "Let me hold your hand, Greta—may I say Greta?—there," and her fingers closed on Greta's with a convulsive grasp.

The operation began. Mercy held her breath. She had the stubborn north-country blood in her. Once only a sigh escaped. There was a dead silence.

In two or three minutes the doctor said, "Just another minute, and all will be over."

At the next instant Greta felt her hand held with a grasp of iron.

"Doctor, doctor, I can see you," cried Mercy, and her words came in gusts.

"Be quiet," said the doctor in a stern voice. In half a minute more the linen bandages were being wrapped tightly over Mercy's eyes.

"Doctor, dear doctor, let me see my boy!" cried Mercy.

"Be quiet, I say," said the doctor again.

"Dear doctor, my dear doctor, only one peep—one little peep. I saw your face—let me see my Ralphie's."

"Not yet, it is not safe."

"But only for a moment. Don't put the bandage on for one moment. Just think, doctor, I have never seen my boy; I've seen other people's children, but never once my own, own darling. Oh, dear doctor—"

"You are exciting yourself. Listen to me: if you don't behave yourself now you may never see your child."

"Yes, yes, I will behave myself; I will be very good. Only don't shut me up in darkness again until I see my boy. Greta, bring him to me. Listen, I hear his breathing. Go for my darling! The kind doctor won't be angry with you. Tell him that if I see my child it will cure me. I know it will."

Greta's eyes were swimming in tears.

"Rest quiet, Mercy. Everything may be lost if you disturb yourself now, my dear."

The doctors were wrapping bandage over bandage, and fixing them firmly at the back of their patient's head.

"Now listen again," said one of them: "This bandage must be kept over your eyes for a week."

"A week—a whole week? Oh, doctor, you might as well say forever."

"I say a week. And if you should ever remove it—"

"Not for an instant? Not raise it a very little?"

"If you ever remove it for an instant, or raise it ever so little, you will assuredly lose your sight forever. Remember that."

"Oh, doctor, it is terrible. Why did you not tell me so before? Oh this is worse than blindness! Think of the temptation, and I have never seen my boy!"

The doctor had fixed the bandage, and his voice was less stern, but no less resolute.

"You must obey me," he said; "I will come again this day week, and then you shall see your child, and your father, and this young lady, and everybody. But mind, if you don't obey me, you will never see anything. You will have one glance of your little boy, and then be blind forever, or perhaps—yes, perhaps *die*."

Mercy lay quiet for a moment. Then she said, in a low voice:

"Dear doctor, you must forgive me. I am very wilful, and I promised to be so good. I will not touch the bandage. No, for the sake of my little boy, I will never, never touch it. You shall come yourself and take it off, and then I shall see him."

The doctors went away. Greta remained all that night in the cottage.

"You are happy now, Mercy?" said Greta.

"Oh yes," said Mercy. "Just think, only a week! And he must be so beautiful by this time."

When Greta took the child to her at sunset, there was an ineffable joy in her pale face, and next morning, when Greta awoke, Mercy was singing softly to herself in the sunrise.

III

Greta stayed with Mercy until noon that day, begging, entreating, and finally commanding her to lie quiet in bed, while she herself dressed and fed the child, and cooked and cleaned, in spite of the Laird Fisher's protestations. When all was done, and the old charcoal-burner had gone out on the hills, Greta picked up the little fellow in her arms and went to Mercy's room. Mercy was alert to every sound, and in an instant was sitting up in bed. Her face beamed, her parted lips smiled, her delicate fingers plucked nervously at the counterpane.

"How brightsome it is to-day, Greta," she said. "I'm sure the sun must be shining."

The window was open, and a soft breeze floated through the sun's rays into the room. Mercy inclined her head aside, and added, "Ah, you young rogue, you; you are there, are you? Give him to me, the rascal!" The rogue was set down in his mother's arms, and she proceeded to punish his rascality with a shower of kisses. "How bonny his cheeks must be; they will be just like two ripe apples," and forthwith there fell another shower of kisses. Then she babbled over the little one, and lisped, and stammered, and nodded her head in his face, and blew little puffs of breath into his hair, and tickled him until he laughed and crowed and rolled and threw up his legs; and then she kissed his limbs and extremities in a way that mothers have, and finally imprisoned one of his feet by putting it ankle-deep into her mouth. "Would you ever think a foot could be so tiny, Greta?" she said. And the little one plunged about and clambered laboriously up its mother's breast, and more than once plucked at the white bandage about her head. "No, no, Ralphie must not touch," said Mercy with sudden gravity. "Only think, Ralphie pet, one week—only one—nay, less—only six days now, and then—oh, then—!" A long hug, and the little fellow's boisterous protest against the convulsive pressure abridged the mother's prophecy.

All at once Mercy's manner changed. She turned toward Greta, and said, "I will not touch the bandage, no, never; but if Ralphie tugged at it, and it fell—would that be breaking my promise?"

Greta saw what was in her heart.

"I'm afraid it would, dear," she said, but there was a tremor in her voice.

Mercy sighed audibly.

"Just think, it would be only Ralphie. The kind doctors could not be angry with my little child. I would say, 'It was the boy,' and they would smile and say, 'Ah, that is different.'"

"Give me the little one," said Greta with emotion.

Mercy drew the child closer, and there was a pause.

"I was very wrong, Greta," she said in a low tone. "Oh! you would not think what a fearful thing came into my mind a minute ago. Take my Ralphie. Just imagine, my own innocent baby tempted me."

As Greta reached across the bed to lift the child out of his mother's lap, the little fellow was struggling to communicate, by help of a limited vocabulary, some wondrous intelligence of recent events that somewhat overshadowed his little existence. "Puss—dat," many times repeated, was further explained by one chubby forefinger with its diminutive finger nail pointed to the fat back of the other hand.

"He means that the little cat has scratched him," said Greta. "But bless the mite, he is pointing to the wrong hand."

"Puss—dat," continued the child, and peered up into his mother's sightless face. Mercy was all tears in an instant. She had borne yesterday's operation without a groan, but now the scratch on her child's hand went to her heart like a stab.

"Lie quiet, Mercy," said Greta; "it will be gone to-morrow."

"Go-on," echoed the little chap, and pointed out at the window.

"The darling, how he picks up every word!" said Greta.

"He means the horse," explained Mercy.

"Go-on—man—go-on," prattled the little one, with a child's in-difference to all conversation except his own.

"Bless the love, he must remember the doctor and his horse," said Greta.

Mercy was putting her lips to the scratch on the little hand.

"Oh, Greta, I am very childish; but a mother's heart melts like butter."

"Batter," echoed the child, and wriggled out of Greta's arms to the ground, where he forthwith clambered on to the stool, and possessed himself of a slice of bread which lay on the table at the bedside. Then the fair curly head disappeared like glint of sunlight through the door to the kitchen.

"What shall I care if other mothers see my child? I shall see him too," said Mercy, and she sighed. "Yes," she added, softly, "his hands and his eyes and his feet, and his soft hair."

"Try to sleep an hour or two, dear," said Greta, "and then perhaps you may get up this afternoon—only *perhaps*, you know, but we'll see."

"Yes, Greta, yes. How kind you are."

"You will be kinder to me some day," said Greta very tenderly.

"How very selfish I am. But then it is so hard not to be selfish when you are a mother. Only fancy, I never think of myself as Mercy now. No, never. I'm just Ralphie's mama. When Ralphie came, Mercy must have died in some way. That's very silly, isn't it? Only it does seem true."

"Man—go-on—batter," was heard from the kitchen, mingled with the patter of tiny feet.

"Listen to him. How tricksome he is! And you should hear him cry 'Oh!' You would say, 'That child has had an eye knocked out.' And then, in a minute, behold he is laughing once more. There, I'm selfish again; but I will make up for it some day, if God is good."

"Yes, Mercy, He is good," said Greta.

Her arm rested on the door-jamb, and her head dropped on to it; her eyes swam. Did it seem at that moment as if God had been very good to these two women?

"Greta," said Mercy, and her voice fell to a whisper, "do you think Ralphie is like—anybody?"

"Yes, dear, he is like you."

There was a pause. Then Mercy's hand strayed from under the bedclothes and plucked at Greta's gown.

"Do you think," she asked, in a voice all but inaudible, "that father knows who it is?"

"I can not say—*we* have never told him."

"Nor I—he never asked, never once—only, you know, he gave up his work at the mine, and went back to the charcoal-pit when Ralphie came. But he never said a word."

Greta did not answer. At that moment the bedroom door was pushed open with a little lordly bang, and the great wee man entered with his piece of bread insecurely on one prong of a fork.

"Toas'," he explained complacently, "toas'," and walked up to the empty grate and stretched his arm over the fender at the cold bars.

"Why, there's no fire for toast, you darling goose," said Greta, catching him in her arms, much to his masculine vexation.

Mercy had risen on an elbow, and her face was full of the yearning of the blind. Then she lay back.

"Never mind," she said to herself in a faltering voice, "let me lie quiet and *think* of all his pretty ways."

IV

G reta returned home toward noon, laughing and crying a little to herself as she walked, for she was full of a dear delicious envy. She was thinking that she could take all the shame and all the pain for all the joy of Mercy's motherhood.

God had given Greta no children.

Hugh Ritson came in to their early dinner and she told him how things went at the cottage of the old Laird Fisher. Only once before had she mentioned Mercy or the child, and he looked confused and awkward. After the meal was over he tried to say something which had been on his mind for weeks.

"But if anything should happen after all," he began, "and Mercy should not recover—or if she should ever want to go anywhere—might we not take—would you mind, Greta—I mean it might even help her— you see," he said, breaking down nearly, "there is the child, it's a sort of duty, you know—and then a good home and upbringing—"

"Don't tempt me," said Greta. "I've thought of it a hundred times."

About five o'clock the same evening a knock came to the door, and old Laird Fisher entered. His manner was more than usually solemn and constrained.

"I's coom't to say as ma lass's wee thing is taken badly," he said, "and rayder suddent."

Greta rose from her seat and put on her hat and cloak. She was hastening down the road while the charcoal-burner was still standing in the middle of the floor.

When Greta reached the old charcoal-burner's cottage, the little one was lying in a drowsy state in Mercy's arms. Its breathing seemed difficult; sometimes it started in terror; it was feverish and suffered thirst. The mother's wistful face was bent down on it with an indescribable expression. There were only the trembling lips to tell of the sharp struggle that was going on within. But the yearning for a sight of the little flushed countenance, the tearless appeal for but one glimpse of the drowsy little eyes, the half-articulate cry of a mother's heart against the fate that made the child she had suckled at her breast a stranger, whose very features she might not know—all this was written in that blind face.

"Is he pale?" said Mercy. "Is he sleeping? He does not talk now, but only starts and cries, and sometimes coughs."

"When did this begin?" asked Greta.

"Toward four o'clock. He had been playing, and I noticed that he breathed heavily, and then he came to me to be nursed. Is he awake now? Listen."

The little one in its restless drowsiness was muttering faintly, "Man—go-on—batter—toas'."

"The darling is talking in his sleep, isn't he?" said Mercy.

Then there was a ringing, brassy cough.

"It is croup," thought Greta.

She closed the window, lighted a fire, placed the kettle so that the steam might enter the room, then wrung flannels out of hot water, and wrapped them about the child's neck. She stayed all that night at the cottage, and sat up with the little one and nursed it. Mercy could not be persuaded to go to bed, but she was very quiet. It had not yet taken hold of her that the child was seriously ill. He was drowsy and a little feverish, his pulse beat fast and he coughed hard sometimes, but he would be better in the morning. Oh, yes, he would soon be well again, and tearing up the flowers in the garden.

Toward midnight the pulse fell rapidly, the breathing became quieter, and the whole nature seemed to sink. Mercy listened with her ear bent down at the child's mouth, and a smile of ineffable joy spread itself over her face.

"Bless him, he is sleeping so calmly," she said.

Greta did not answer.

"The 'puss' and the 'man' don't darken his little life so much now," continued Mercy cheerily.

"No, dear," said Greta, in as strong a voice as she could summon.

"All will be well with my darling boy soon, will it not?"

"Yes, dear," said Greta, with a struggle.

Happily Mercy could not read the other answer in her face.

Mercy had put her sensitive fingers on the child's nose, and was touching him lightly about the mouth.

"Greta," she said in a startled whisper, "does he look pinched?"

"A little," said Greta quietly.

"And his skin—is it cold and clammy?"

"We must give him another hot flannel," said Greta.

Mercy sat at the bedside, and said nothing for an hour. Then all at once, and in a strange, harsh voice, she said:

"I wish God had not made Ralphie so winsome."

Greta started at the words, but made no answer.

The daylight came early. As the first gleams of gray light came in at the window, Greta turned to where Mercy sat in silence. It was a sad face that she saw in the mingled yellow light of the dying lamp and the gray of the dawn.

Mercy spoke again.

"Greta, do you remember what Mistress Branthet said when her baby died last back end gone twelvemonth?"

Greta looked up quickly at the bandaged eyes.

"What?" she asked.

"Well, Parson Christian tried to comfort her and said: 'Your baby is now an angel in Paradise,' and she turned on him with: 'Shaf on your angels—I want none on 'em—I want my little girl.'"

Mercy's voice broke into a sob.

Toward ten o'clock the doctor came. He had been detained. Very sorry to disoblige Mrs. Ritson, but fact was old Mr. de Broadthwaite had an attack of lumbago, complicated by a bout of toothache, and everybody knew he was most exacting. Young person's baby ill? Feverish, restless, starts in its sleep, and cough? Ah, croupy cough—yes, croup, true croup, not spasmodic. Let him see, how old? A year and a half? Ah, bad, very. Most frequent in second year of infancy. Dangerous, highly so. Forms a membrane that occludes air-passages. Often ends in convulsions, and child suffocates. Sad, very. Let him see again. How long since the attack began? Yesterday at four. Ah, far gone, far. The great man soon vanished, leaving behind him a harmless preparation of aconite and ipecacuanha.

Mercy had heard all, and her pent-up grief broke out in sobs.

"Oh, to think I shall hear my Ralphie no more, and to know his white cold face is looking up from a coffin, while other children are playing in the sunshine and chasing the butterflies! No, no, it can not be; God will not let it come to pass; I will pray to Him and He will save my child. Why, He can do anything, and He has all the world. What is my little baby boy to Him? He will not let it be taken from me."

Greta's heart was too full for speech. But she might weep in silence, and none there would know. Mercy stretched across the bed, and, tenderly folding the child in her arms, she lifted him up, and then went down on her knees.

"Merciful Father," she said in a childish voice of sweet confidence, "this is my baby, my Ralphie, and I love him so dearly. You would never think how much I love him. But he is ill, and doctor says he may die. Oh, dear Father, only think what it would be to say, 'His little face is gone.' And then I have never seen him. You will not take him away until his mother sees him. So soon, too. Only five days more. Why, it is quite close. Not to-morrow, nor the next day, nor the next, but the day after that."

She put in many another childlike plea, and then rose with a smile on her pale lips and replaced the little one on his pillow.

"How patient he is," she said. "He can't say 'Thank you,' but I'm sure his eyes are speaking. Let me feel." She put her finger lightly on the child's lids. "No, they are shut; he must be sleeping. Oh, dear, he sleeps very much. Is he gaining color? How quiet he is. If he would only say, 'Mama!' How I wish I could see him!"

She was very quiet for a while, and then plucked at Greta's gown suddenly.

"Greta," she said eagerly, "something tells me that if I could only see Ralphie I should save him."

Greta started up in terror. "No, no, no; you must not think of it," she said.

"But something whispered it. It must have been God himself. You know we ought to obey God always."

"Mercy, it was not God who said that. It was your own heart. You must not heed it."

"I'm sure it was God," said Mercy. "And I heard it quite plain."

"Mercy, my darling, think what you are saying. Think what it is you wish to do. If you do it you will be blind forever."

"But I shall have saved my Ralphie."

"No, no; you will not."

"Will he not be saved, Greta?"

"Only our heavenly Father knows."

"Well, He whispered it in my heart. And, as you say, He knows best."

Greta was almost distraught with fear. The noble soul in her would not allow her to appeal to Mercy's gratitude against the plea of maternal love. But she felt that all her happiness hung on that chance. If Mercy regained her sight, all would be well with her and hers; but if she lost it the future must be a blank.

The day wore slowly on, and the child sank and sank. At evening the old charcoal-burner returned, and went into the bedroom. He stood a moment and looked down at the pinched little face, and when the child's eyes opened drowsily for a moment he put his withered forefinger into its palm; but there was no longer a responsive clasp of the chubby hand.

The old man's lips quivered behind his white beard.

"It were a winsome wee thing," he said faintly, and then turned away.

He left his supper untouched, and went into the porch. There he sat on a bench and whittled a blackthorn stick. The sun was sinking over the head of the Eal Crag; the valley lay deep in a purple haze; only the bald top of Cat Bells stood out bright in the glory of the passing day. A gentle breeze came up from the south, and the young corn chattered with its multitudinous tongues in a field below. The dog lay at the charcoal-burner's feet, blinking in the sun and snapping lazily at a buzzing fly.

The little life within was ebbing away. No longer racked by the ringing cough, the loud breathing became less frequent and more harsh. Mercy lifted the child from the bed, and sat with it before the fire. Greta saw its eyes open, and at the same moment she saw the lips move slightly, but she heard nothing.

"He is calling his mama," said Mercy, with her ear bent toward the child's mouth.

There was a silence for a long time. Mercy pressed the child to her breast; its close presence seemed to soothe her.

Greta stood and looked down; she saw the little lips move once more, but again she heard no sound.

"He is calling his mama," repeated Mercy wistfully, "and oh, he seems such a long way off."

Once again the little lips moved.

"He is calling me," said Mercy, listening intently; and she grew restless and excited. "He is going away. I can hear him. He is far off. Ralphie, Ralphie!" She had lifted the child up to her face. "Ralphie, Ralphie!" she cried.

"Give me the baby, Mercy," said Greta.

But the mother clung to it with a convulsive grasp.

"Ralphie, Ralphie, Ralphie. . ."

There was a sudden flash of some white thing. In an instant the bandage had fallen from Mercy's head, and she was peering down into the child's face with wild eyes.

"Ralphie, Ralphie!. . . *Hugh!*" she cried.

The mother had seen her babe at last, and in that instant she had recognized the features of its father.

At the next moment the angel of God passed through that troubled house, and the child lay dead at the mother's breast.

Mercy saw it all, and her impassioned mood left her. She rose to her feet quietly, and laid the little one in the bed. There was never a sigh more, never a tear. Only her face was ashy pale, and her whitening lips quivered.

"Greta," she said, very slowly, "good-by! All is over now."

She spoke of herself as if her days were already ended and past; as if her own orb of life had been rounded by the brief span of the little existence that lay finished on the bed.

"When they come in the morning early—very early—and find us here, my boy and me, don't let them take him away from me, Greta. We should go together—yes, both together; that's only right, with Ralphie at my bosom."

The bandage lay at her feet. Her eyes were very red and heavy. Their dim light seemed to come from far away.

"Only that," she said, and her voice softened, "My Ralphie is in heaven."

Then she hid her face in her hands, and cried out loud, "But I prayed to God that I might see my child on earth. Oh, how I prayed! And God heard my prayer and answered it—but see! *I saw him die.*"

END OF "THE BLIND MOTHER"

THE LAST CONFESSION

I

Father, do not leave me. Wait! only a little longer. You can not absolve me? I am not penitent? How *can* I be penitent? I do not regret it? How *can* I regret it? I would do it again? How could I help *but* do it again?

Yes, yes, I know, I know! Who knows it so well as I? It is written in the tables of God's law: *Thou shalt do no murder!* But was it murder? Was it crime? Blood? Yes, it was the spilling of blood. Blood will have blood, you say. But is there no difference? Hear me out. Let me speak. It is hard to remember all now—and here—lying here—but listen—only listen. Then tell me if I did wrong. No, tell me if God Himself will not justify me—ay, justify me—though I outraged His edict. Blasphemy? Ah, father, do not go! Father!—

Speak, my son. I will listen. It is my duty. Speak.

It is less than a year since my health broke down, but the soul lives fast, and it seems to me like a lifetime. I had overworked myself miserably. My life as a physician in London had been a hard one, but it was not my practise that had wrecked me. How to perform that operation on the throat was the beginning of my trouble. You know what happened. I mastered my problem, and they called the operation by my name. It has brought me fame; it has made me rich; it has saved a thousand lives, and will save ten thousand more, and yet I—I—for taking one life—one—under conditions—

Father, bear with me. I will tell all. My nerves are burned out. Gloom, depression, sleeplessness, prostration, sometimes collapse, a consuming fire within, a paralyzing frost without—you know what it is—we call it neurasthenia.

I watched the progress of my disease and gave myself the customary treatment. Hygiene, diet, drugs, electricity, I tried them all. But neither dumbbells nor Indian clubs, neither walking nor riding, neither liberal food nor doses of egg and brandy, neither musk nor ergot nor antipyrin, neither faradization nor galvanization availed to lift the black shades that hung over me day and night, and made the gift of life a mockery. I knew why. My work possessed me like a fever. I could neither do it to my content nor leave it undone. I was drawing water in a sieve.

My wife sent for Gull. Full well I knew what he would advise. It was rest. I must take six months' absolute holiday, and, in order to cut myself off entirely from all temptations to mental activity, I must leave London and go abroad. Change of scene, of life, and of habit, new peoples, new customs, new faiths, and a new climate—these separately and together, with total cessation of my usual occupations, were to banish a long series of functional derangements which had for their basis the exhaustion of the sympathetic nervous system.

I was loth to go. Looking back upon my condition, I see that my reluctance was justified. To launch a creature who was all nerves into the perpetual, if trifling, vexations of travel was a mistake, a folly, a madness. But I did not perceive this; I was thinking only of my home and the dear souls from whom I must be separated. During the seven years of our married life my wife had grown to be more than the object of my love. That gentle soothing, that soft healing which the mere presence of an affectionate woman who is all strength and courage may bring to a man who is wasted by work or worry, my wife's presence had long brought to me, and I shrank from the thought of scenes where she could no longer move about me, meeting my wishes and anticipating my wants.

This was weakness, and I knew it; but I had another weakness which I did not know. My boy, a little son of six years of age the day before I set sail, was all the world to me. Paternal love may eat up all the other passions. It was so in my case. The tyranny of my affection for my only child was even more constant and unrelenting than the tyranny of my work. Nay, the two were one: for out of my instinct as a father came my strength as a doctor. The boy had suffered from a throat trouble from his birth. When he was a babe I delivered him from a fierce attack of it, and when he was four I brought him back from the jaws of death. Thus twice I had saved his life, and each time that life had become dearer to me. But too well I knew that the mischief was beaten down, and not conquered. Some day it would return with awful virulence. To meet that terror I wrought by day and night. No slave ever toiled so hard. I denied myself rest, curtailed my sleep, and stole from tranquil reflection and repose half-hours and quarter-hours spent in the carriage going from patient to patient. The attack might come suddenly, and I must be prepared. I was working against time.

You know what happened. The attack did not come; my boy continued well, but my name became known and my discovery established. The weakness of my own child had given the bent to my studies. If I had mastered my subject it was my absorbing love of my little one that gave me the impulse and direction.

But I had paid my penalty. My health was a wreck, and I must leave everything behind me. If it had been possible to take my wife and boy along with me, how different the end might have been! Should I be lying here now—here on this bed—with you, father, you?—

We spent our boy's birthday with what cheer we could command. For my wife it seemed to be a day of quiet happiness, hallowed by precious memories—the dearest and most delicious that a mother ever knew—of the babyhood of her boy—his pretty lisp, his foolish prattle, his funny little ways and sayings—and sweetened by the anticipation of the health that was to return to me as the result of rest and change. The child himself was bright and gamesome, and I for my part gave way to some reckless and noisy jollity.

Thus the hours passed until bedtime, and then, as I saw the little fellow tucked up in his crib, it crossed my mind for a moment that he looked less well than usual. Such fancies were common to me, and I knew from long experience that it was folly to give way to them. To do so at that time must have been weakness too pitiful for my manhood. I had already gone far enough for my own self-respect. To my old colleague and fellow-student, Granville Wenman, I had given elaborate instructions for all possible contingencies.

If *this* happened he was to do *that*; if *that* happened he was to do *this*. In case of serious need he was to communicate with me by the swiftest means available, for neither the width of the earth nor the wealth of the world, nor the loss of all chances of health or yet life, should keep me from hastening home if the one hope of my heart was in peril. Wenman had smiled a little as in pity of the morbidity that ran out to meet so many dangers. I did not heed his good-natured compassion or contempt, whatever it was, for I knew he had no children. I had reconciled myself in some measure to my absence from home, and before my little man was awake in the morning I was gone from the house.

It had been arranged that I should go to Morocco. Wenman had suggested that country out of regard to the freshness of its life and people. The East in the West, the costumes of Arabia, the faiths of Mohammed and of Moses, a primitive form of government, and a social life that might have been proper to the land of Canaan in the days of Abraham—such had seemed to him and others to be an atmosphere of novelty that was likely to bring spring and elasticity to the overstretched mind and nerves of a victim of the civilization of our tumultuous century. But not in all the world could fate have ferreted out for me a scene more certain to develop the fever and fret of my natural temperament. Had the choice fallen on any other place, any dead or dying country, any corner of God's earth but that blighted and desolate land—

Ah! bear with me, bear with me.

I know it, my son. It is near to my own country. My home is in Spain. I came to your England from Seville. Go on.

I sailed to Gibraltar by a P. and O. steamer from Tilbury, and the tender that took my wife back to the railway pier left little in my new condition to interest me. You know what it is to leave home in search of health. If hope is before you, regret is behind. When I stood on the upper deck that night, alone, and watched the light of the Eddystone dying down over the dark waters, it seemed to me that success had no solace, and fame no balm, and riches no safety or content. One reflection alone sufficed to reconcile me to where I was—the work that had brought me there was done neither for fame nor for riches, but at the prompting of the best of all earthly passions—or what seemed to be the best.

Three days passed, and beyond casual words I had spoken to no one on the ship. But on the fourth day, as we sailed within sight of Finisterre in a calm sea, having crossed the Bay with comfort, the word went round that a storm-signal was hoisted on the cape. No one who has gone through an experience such as that is likely to forget it. Everybody on deck, the blanched faces, the hushed voices, the quick whispers, the eager glances around, the interrogations of the officers on duty, and their bantering answers belied by their anxious looks, then the darkening sky, the freshening breeze, the lowering horizon, the tingling gloomy atmosphere creeping down from the mastheads, and the air of the whole ship, above and below, charged, as it were, with sudden electricity. It is like nothing else in life except the bugle-call in camp, telling those who lie smoking and drinking about the fires that the enemy is coming, and is near.

I was standing on the quarterdeck watching the Lascars stowing sails, battening down the hatches, clewing the lines, and making everything snug, when a fellow-passenger whom I had not observed before stepped up and spoke. His remark was a casual one, and it has gone from my memory. I think it had reference to the native seamen, and was meant as a jest upon their lumbering slowness, which suggested pitiful thoughts to him of what their capacity must be in a storm. But the air of the man much more than his words aroused and arrested my attention. It was that of one whose spirits had been quickened by the new sense of danger. He laughed, his eyes sparkled, his tongue rolled out his light remarks with a visible relish. I looked at the man and saw that he had the soul of a war-horse. Tall, slight, dark, handsome, with bushy beard, quivering nostrils, mobile mouth, and eyes of fire, alive in every fibre, and full of unconquerable energy. He appeared to be a man of thirty to thirty-five, but proved to be no more than four-and-twenty. I learned afterward that he was an American, and was traveling for love of adventure.

That night we flew six hours before the storm, but it overtook our ship at last. What befell us then in the darkness of that rock-bound coast I did not know until morning. Can you believe it? I took my usual dose of a drug prescribed to me for insomnia, and lay down to sleep. When I went up on deck in the late dawn of the following day—the time was spring—the wind had slackened, and the ship was rolling and swinging along in a sea that could not be heard above the beat and thud of the engines. Only the memory of last night's tempest lay around in sullen wave and sky—only there, and in the quarters down below of the native seamen of our ship.

The first face I encountered was that of the American. He had been on deck all night, and he told me what had happened. Through the dark hours the storm had been terrible, and when the first dead light of dawn had crept across from the east the ship had been still tossing in great white billows. Just then a number of Lascars had been ordered aloft on some urgent duty—I know not what—and a sudden gust had swept one of them from a cross-tree into the sea. Efforts had been made to rescue him, the engines had been reversed, boats put out and life-buoys thrown into the water, but all in vain. The man had been swept away; he was gone and the ship had steamed on.

The disaster saddened me inexpressibly. I could see the Lascar fall from the rigging, catch the agonizing glance of the white eyes in his black face as he was swept past on the crest of a wave, and watch his outstretched arms as he sank to his death down and down and down. It seemed to me an iniquity that while this had happened I had slept. Perhaps the oversensitive condition of my nerves was at fault, but indeed I felt that, in his way, in his degree, within the measure of his possibilities, that poor fellow of another skin, another tongue, with whom I had exchanged no word of greeting, had that day given his life for my life.

How much of such emotion I expressed at the time it is hard to remember now, but that the American gathered the bent of my feelings was clear to me by the pains he was at to show that they were uncalled for, and unnatural, and false. What was life? I had set too great a store by it. The modern reverence for life was eating away the finest instincts of man's nature. Life was not the most sacred of our possessions. Duty, justice, truth, these were higher things.

So he talked that day and the next until, from thoughts of the loss of the Lascar, we had drifted far into wider and more perilous speculations. The American held to his canon. War was often better than peace, and open massacre than corrupt tranquillity. We wanted some of the robust spirit of the Middle Ages in these our piping days. The talk turned on the persecution of the Jews in Russia. The American defended it—a stern people was purging itself of an alien element which, like an interminate tapeworm, had been preying on its vitals. The remedy was drastic but necessary; life was lost, but also life was saved.

Then coming to closer quarters we talked of murder. The American held to the doctrine of Sterne. It was a hard case that the laws of the modern world should not have made any manner of difference between murdering an honest man and only executing a scoundrel. These things should always be rated ad valorem. As for blood spilled in self-defense, it was folly to talk of it as crime. Even the laws of my own effeminate land justified the man who struck down the arm that was raised to kill him; and the mind that reckoned such an act as an offense was morbid and diseased.

Such opinions were repugnant to me, and I tried to resist them. There was a sanctity about human life which no man should dare to outrage. God gave it, and only God should take it away. As for the government of the world, let it be for better or for worse, it was in God's hands, and God required the help of no man.

My resistance was useless. The American held to his doctrine; it was good to take life in a good cause, and if it was good for the nation, it was good for the individual man. The end was all.

I fenced these statements with what force I could command, and I knew not how strongly my adversary had assailed me. Now, I know too well that his opinions sank deep into my soul. Only too well I know it now—now that—

We arrived at Gibraltar the following morning, and going up on deck in the empty void of air that follows on the sudden stopping of a ship's engines, I found the American, amid a group of swarthy Gibraltarians, bargaining for a boat to take him to the Mole. It turned out that he was going to Morocco also, and we hired a boat together.

The morning was clear and cold; the great broad rock looked whiter and starker and more like a gigantic oyster-shell than ever against the blue of the sky. There would be no steamer for Tangier until the following day, and we were to put up at the Spanish hotel called the Calpe.

Immediately on landing I made my way to the post-office to despatch a telegram home announcing my arrival, and there I found two letters, which, having come overland, arrived in advance of me. One of them was from Wenman, telling me that he had called at Wimpole Street the morning after my departure and found all well at my house; and also enclosing a resolution of thanks and congratulation from my colleagues of the College of Surgeons in relation to my recent labors, which were said to be "memorable in the cause of humanity and science."

The other letter was from my wife, a sweet, affectionate little note, cheerful yet tender, written on her return from Tilbury, hinting that the dear old house looked just a trifle empty and as if somehow it missed something, but that our boy was up and happy with a new toy that I had left for him as a consolation on his awakening—a great elephant that worked its trunk and roared. "I have just asked our darling," wrote my wife, "what message he would like to send you. 'Tell papa,' he answers, 'I'm all right, and Jumbo's all right, and is he all right, and will he come werry quick, and see him grunting?'"

That night at the Calpe I had some further talk with the American. Young as he was he had been a great Eastern traveler. Egypt, Arabia, Syria, the Holy Land—he knew them all. For his forthcoming sojourn in Morocco he had prepared himself with elaborate care. The literature of travel in Barbary is voluminous, but he had gone through the best of it. With the faith of Islam he had long been familiar, and of the corrupt and tyrannical form of government of Mulai el Hassan and his kaids and kadis he had an intimate knowledge. He had even studied the language of the Moorish people—the Moroccan Arabic, which is a dialect of the language of the Koran—and so that he might hold intercourse with the Sephardic Jews also, who people the Mellahs of Morocco, he had mastered the Spanish language as well.

This extensive equipment, sufficient to start a crusade or to make a revolution, was meant to do more than provide him with adventure.

His intention was to see the country and its customs, to observe the manners of the people and the ordinances of their religion. "I shall get into the palaces and the prisons of the Kasbahs," he said; "yes, and the mosques and the saints' houses, and the harems also."

Little as I knew then of the Moors and their country, I foresaw the dangers of such an enterprise, and I warned him against it. "You will get yourself into awkward corners," I said.

"Yes," he said, "and I shall get myself out of them."

I remembered his doctrine propounded on the ship, and I saw that he was a man of resolution, but I said, "Remember, you are going to the land of this people for amusement alone. It is not necessity that thrusts you upon their prejudice, their superstition, their fanaticism."

"True," he said, "but if I get into trouble among them it will not be my amusements but my liberty or my life that will be in danger."

"Then in such a case you will stick at nothing to plow your way out?"

"Nothing."

I laughed, for my mind refused to believe him, and we laughed noisily together, with visions of bloody daggers before the eyes of both.

Father, my *heart* believed: silently, secretly, unconsciously, it drank in the poison of his thought—drank it in—ay—

Next day, about noon, we sailed for Tangier. Our ship was the *Jackal*, a little old iron steam-tug, battered by time and tempest, clamped and stayed at every side, and just holding together as by the grace of God. The storm which we had outraced from Finisterre had now doubled Cape St. Vincent, and the sea was rolling heavily in the Straits. We saw nothing of this until we had left the bay and were standing out from Tarifa; nor would it be worthy of mention now but that it gave me my first real understanding of the tremendous hold that the faith or the fanaticism of the Moorish people—call it what you will—has upon their characters and lives.

The channel at that point is less than twenty miles wide, but we were more than five hours crossing it. Our little crazy craft labored terribly in the huge breakers that swept inward from the Atlantic. Pitching until the foredeck was covered, rolling until her boats dipped in the water, creaking, shuddering, leaping, she had enough to do to keep afloat.

With the American I occupied the bridge between the paddle-boxes, which served as a saloon for first-class passengers; and below us in the open hold of the after-deck a number of Moors sat huddled together among cattle and sheep and baskets of fowl. They were Pilgrims, Hadjis, returning from Mecca by way of Gibraltar, and their behavior during the passage was marvelous in its callousness to the sense of peril. They wrangled, quarreled, snarled at each other, embraced, kissed, laughed together, made futile attempts to smoke their keef-pipes, and quarreled, barked, and bleated again.

"Surely," I said, "these people are either wondrously brave or they have no sense of the solemnity of death."

"Neither," said the American; "they are merely fatalists by virtue of their faith. 'If it is not now, it is to come; if it is not to come then it is now.'"

"There is a sort of bravery in that," I answered.

"And cowardice, too," said the American.

The night had closed in when we dropped anchor by the ruins of the Mole at Tangier, and I saw no more of the white town than I had seen of it from the Straits. But if my eyes failed in the darkness my other senses served me only too well. The shrieking and yelping of the boatloads of Moors and negroes who clambered aboard to relieve us of our luggage, the stench of the town sewers that emptied into the bay— these were my first impressions of the gateway to the home of Islam.

The American went through the turmoil with composure and an air of command, and having seen to my belongings as well as his own, passing them through the open office at the water-gate, where two solemn Moors in white sat by the light of candles, in the receipt of customs, he parted from me at the foot of the street that begins with the Grand Mosque, and is the main artery of the town, for he had written for rooms to the hotel called the Villa de France, and I, before leaving England, had done the same to the hotel called the Continental.

Thither I was led by a barefooted courier in white jellab and red tarboosh, amid sights and sounds of fascinating strangeness: the low drone of men's voices singing their evening prayers in the mosques, the tinkling of the bells of men selling water out of goats' skins, the "Allah" of blind beggars crouching at the gates, the "Arrah" of the mule drivers, and the hooded shapes going by in the gloom or squatting in the red glare of the cafés without windows or doors and open to the streets.

I met the American in the Sôk—the market-place—the following day, and he took me up to his hotel to see some native costumes which he had bought by way of preparations for his enterprise. They were haiks and soolhams, jellabs, kaftans, slippers, rosaries, korans, sashes, satchels, turbans, and tarbooshes—blue, white, yellow, and red—all right and none too new, for he had purchased them not at the bazaars, but from the son of a learned Moor, a Tàleb, who had been cast into a prison by a usurer Jew.

"In these," said he, "I mean to go everywhere, and I'll defy the devil himself to detect me."

"Take care," I said, "take care."

He laughed and asked me what my own plans were. I told him that I would remain in Tangier until I received letters from home, and then push on toward Fez.

"I'll see you there," he said; "but if I do not hail you, please do not know me. Good-by."

"Good-by," I said, and so we parted.

I stayed ten days longer in Tangier, absorbed in many reflections, of which the strangest were these two: first, the Moors were the most religious people in the world, and next, that they were the most wickedly irreligious and basely immoral race on God's earth. I was prompted to the one by observations of the large part which Allah appears to play in all affairs of Moorish life, and to the other by clear proof of the much larger part which the devil enacts in Allah's garments. On the one side prayers, prayers, prayers, the moodden, the moodden, the moodden, the mosque, the mosque, the mosque. "Allah" from the mouths of the beggars, "Allah" from the lips of the merchants, "Mohammed" on the inscriptions at the gate, the "Koran" on the scarfs hung out at the bazaars and on the satchels hawked in the streets. And on the other side shameless lying, cheating, usury, buying and selling of justice, cruelty and inhumanity; raw sores on the backs of the asses, blood in the streets, blood, blood, blood everywhere and secret corruption indescribable.

Nevertheless I concluded that my nervous malady must have given me the dark glasses through which everything looked so foul, and I resolved, in the interests of health, to push on toward Fez as soon as letters arrived from home assuring me that all were well and happy there.

But no letters came, and at the arrival of every fresh mail from Cadiz and from Gibraltar my impatience increased. At length I decided to wait no longer, and, leaving instructions that my letters should be sent on after me to the capital, I called on the English Consul for such official documents as were needful for my journey.

When these had been produced from the Kasbah, and I was equipped for travel, the Consul inquired of me how I liked the Moors and their country. I described my conflicting impressions, and he said both were right in their several ways.

"The religion of the Moor," said he, "is genuine of its kind, though it does not put an end to the vilest Government on earth and the most loathsome immoralities ever practised by man. Islam is a sacred thing to him. He is proud of it, jealous of it, and prepared to die for it. Half his hatred of the unbeliever is fear that the Nazarene or the Jew is eager to show his faith some dishonor. And that," added the Consul, "reminds me to offer you one word of warning: avoid the very shadow of offense to the religion of these people; do not pry into their beliefs; do not take note of their ordinances; pass their mosques and saints' houses with down-cast eyes, if need be; in a word, let Islam alone."

I thanked him for his counsel, and, remembering the American, I inquired what the penalty would be if a foreign subject offended the religion of this people. The Consul lifted his eyebrows and shoulders together, with an eloquence of reply that required no words.

"But might not a stranger," I asked, "do so unwittingly?"

"Truly," he answered, "and so much the worse for his ignorance."

"Is British life, then," I said, "at the mercy of the first ruffian with a dagger? Is there no power in solemn treaties?"

"What are treaties," he said, "against fanaticism? Give the one a wide berth and you'll have small need for the other."

After that he told me something of certain claims just settled for long imprisonment inflicted by the Moorish authorities on men trading under the protection of the British flag. It was an abject story of barbarous cruelty, broken health, shattered lives, and wrecked homes, atoned for after weary procrastination, in the manner of all Oriental courts, by a sorry money payment. The moral of it all was conveyed by the Consul in the one word with which he parted from me at his gate. "Respect the fanaticism of these fanatics," he said, "as you would value your liberty or your life, and keep out of a Moorish prison—remember that, remember that!"

I *did* remember it. Every day of my travels I remembered it. I remembered it at the most awful moment of my life. If I had not remembered it then, should I be lying here now with that—with *that*—behind me! Ah, wait, wait!

Little did I expect when I left the Consul to light so soon upon a terrible illustration of his words. With my guide and interpreter, a Moorish soldier lent to me by the authorities in return for two pesetas (one shilling and ninepence) a day, I strolled into the greater Sôk, the market-place outside the walls. It was Friday, the holy day of the Moslems, somewhere between one and two o'clock in the afternoon, when the body of the Moors having newly returned from their one-hour observances in the mosques, had resumed, according to their wont, their usual occupations. The day was fine and warm, a bright sun was shining, and the Sôk at the time when we entered it was a various and animated scene.

Dense crowds of hooded figures, clad chiefly in white—soiled or dirty white—men in jellabs, women enshrouded in blankets, barefooted girls, boys with shaven polls, water-carriers with their tinkling bells, snake-charmers, story-tellers, jugglers, preachers, and then donkeys, nosing their way through the throng, mules lifting their necks above the people's heads, and camels munching oats and fighting—it was a wilderness of writhing forms and a babel of shrieking noises.

With my loquacious Moor I pushed my way along past booths and stalls until I came to a white-washed structure with a white flag floating over it, that stood near the middle of the market-place. It was a roofless place, about fifteen feet square, and something like a little sheepfold, but having higher walls. Through the open doorway I saw an inner enclosure, out of which a man came forward. He was a wild-eyed creature in tattered garments, and dirty, disheveled, and malevolent of face.

"See," said my guide, "see, my lord, a Moorish saint's house. Look at the flag. So shall my lord know a saint's house. Here rest the bones of Sidi Gali, and that is the saint that guards them. A holy man, yes, a holy man. Moslems pay him tribute. Sacred place, yes, sacred. No Nazarene may enter it. But Moslem, yes, Moslems may fly here for sanctuary. Life to the Moslem, death to the Nazarene. So it is."

My soldier was rattling on in this way when I saw coming in the sunlight down the hillside of which the Sôk is the foot a company of some eight or ten men, whose dress and complexion were unlike those of the people gathered there. They were a band of warlike persons, swarthy, tall, lithe, sinewy, with heads clean shaven save for one long lock that hung from the crown, each carrying a gun with barrel of prodigious length upon his shoulder, and also armed with a long naked Reefian knife stuck in the scarf that served him for a belt.

They were Berbers, the descendants of the race that peopled Barbary before the Moors set foot in it, between whom and the Moors there is a long-continued, suppressed, but ineradicable enmity. From their mountain homes these men had come to the town that day on their pleasure or their business, and as they entered it they were at no pains to conceal their contempt for the townspeople and their doings.

Swaggering along with long strides, they whooped and laughed and plowed their way through the crowd over bread and vegetables spread out on the ground, and the people fell back before them with muttered curses until they were come near to the saint's house, beside which I myself with my guide was standing. Then I saw that the keeper of the saint's house, the half-distraught creature whom I had just observed, was spitting out at them some bitter and venomous words.

Clearly they all heard him, and most of them laughed derisively and pushed on. But one of the number—a young Berber with eyes of fire—drew up suddenly and made some answer in hot and rapid words. The man of the saint's house spoke again, showing his teeth as he did so in a horrible grin; and at the next instant, almost quicker than my eyes could follow the swift movement of his hands, the Berber had plucked his long knife from his belt and plunged it into the keeper's breast.

I saw it all. The man fell at my feet, and was dead in an instant. In another moment the police of the market had laid hold of the murderer, and he was being hauled off to his trial. "Come," whispered my guide, and he led me by short cuts through the narrow lanes to the Kasbah.

In an open alcove of the castle I found two men in stainless blue jellabs and spotless white turbans, squatting on rush mats at either foot of the horse-shoe arch. These were the judges, the Kadi and his Khalifa, sitting in session in the hall of justice.

There was a tumult of many voices and of hurrying feet; and presently the police entered, holding their prisoner between them, and followed by a vast concourse of townspeople. I held my ground in front of the alcove; the Berber was brought up near to my side, and I saw and heard all.

"This man," said one of the police, "killed so-and-so, of Sidi Gali's saint's house."

"When?" said the Kadi.

"This moment," said the police.

"How?" said the Kadi.

"With this knife," said the police.

The knife, stained, and still wet, was handed to the judge. He shook it, and asked the prisoner one question: "Why?"

Then the Berber flung himself on his knees—his shaven head brushed my hand—and began to plead extenuating circumstances. "It is true, my lord, I killed him, but he called me dog and infidel, and spat at me—"

The Kadi gave back the knife and waved his hand. "Take him away," he said.

That was all, as my guide interpreted it. "Come," he whispered again, and he led me by a passage into a sort of closet where a man lay on a mattress. This was the porch to the prison, and the man on the mattress was the jailer. In one wall there was a low door, barred and clamped with iron, and having a round peephole grated across.

At the next instant the police brought in their prisoner. The jailer rattled a big key in the lock, the low door swung open, I saw within a dark den full of ghostly figures dragging chains at their ankles; a foul stench came out of it, the prisoner bent his head and was pushed in, the door slammed back—and that was the end. Everything occurred in no more time than it takes to tell it.

"Is that all his trial?" I asked.

"All," said my guide.

"How long will he lie there?"

"Until death."

"But," I said, "I have heard that a Kadi of your country may be bribed to liberate a murderer."

"Ah, my lord is right," said my guide, "but not the murderer of a saint."

Less than five minutes before I had seen the stalwart young Berber swaggering down the hillside in the afternoon sunshine. Now he was in the gloom of the noisome dungeon, with no hope of ever again looking upon the light of day, doomed to drag out an existence worse than death, and all for what? For taking life? No, no, no—life in that land is cheap, cheaper than it ever was in the Middle Ages—but for doing dishonor to a superstition of the faith of Islam.

I remembered the American, and shuddered at the sight of this summary justice. Next morning, as my tentmen and muleteers were making ready to set out for Fez, my soldier-guide brought me a letter which had come by the French steamer by way of Malaga. It was from home; a brief note from my wife, with no explanation of her prolonged silence, merely saying that all was as usual at Wimpole Street, and not mentioning our boy at all. The omission troubled me, the brevity and baldness of the message filled me with vague concern, and I had half a mind to delay my inland journey. Would that I had done so! Would that I had! Oh, would that I had!

Terrible, my son, terrible! A blighted and desolated land. But even worse than its own people are the renegades it takes from mine. Ah, I knew one such long ago. An outcast, a pariah, a shedder of blood, an apostate. But go on, go on.

II

Father, what voice was it that rang in my ears and cried, "Stay, do not travel; all your past from the beginning until to-day, all your future from to-day until the end, hangs on your action now; go, and your past is a waste, your fame a mockery, your success a reproach; remain, and your future is peace and happiness and content!" What voice, father, what voice?

I shut my ears to it, and six days afterward I arrived at Fez. My journey had impressed two facts upon my mind with startling vividness; first, that the Moor would stick at nothing in his jealousy of the honor of his faith, and next, that I was myself a changed and coarsened man. I was reminded of the one when in El Kassar I saw an old Jew beaten in the open streets because he had not removed his slippers and walked barefoot as he passed the front of a mosque; and again in Wazzan, when I witnessed the welcome given to the Grand Shereef on his return from his home in Tangier to his house in the capital of his province. The Jew was the chief usurer of the town, and had half the Moorish inhabitants in his toils; yet his commercial power had counted for nothing against the honor of Islam. "I," said he to me that night in the Jewish inn, the Fondak, "I, who could clap every man of them in the Kasbah, and their masters with them, for moneys they owe me, I to be treated like a dog by these scurvy sons of Ishmael—God of Jacob!" The Grand Shereef was a drunkard, a gamester, and worse. There was no ordinance of Mohammed which he had not openly outraged, yet because he stood to the people as the descendant of the Prophet, and the father of the faith, they groveled on the ground before him and kissed his robes, his knees, his feet, his stirrups, and the big hoofs of the horse that carried him. As for myself, I realized that the atmosphere of the country had corrupted me, when I took out from my baggage a curved knife in its silver-mounted sheath, which I had bought of a hawker at Tangier, and fixed it prominently in the belt of my Norfolk jacket.

The morning after my arrival in Fez I encountered my American companion of the voyage. Our meeting was a strange one. I had rambled aimlessly with my guide through the new town into the old until I had lighted by chance upon the slave market in front of the ruins of the ancient Grand Mosque, and upon a human auction which was then proceeding. No scene so full of shame had I ever beheld, but the fascination of the spectacle held me, and I stood and watched and listened. The slave being sold was a black girl, and she was beautiful according to the standard of her skin, bareheaded, barefooted, and clad as lightly over her body as decency allowed, so as to reveal the utmost of her charms.

"Now, brothers," cried the salesman, "look, see" (pinching the girl's naked arms and rolling his jeweled fingers from her chin downward over her bare neck on to her bosom), "sound of wind and limb, and with rosy lips, fit for the kisses of a king—how much?"

"A hundred dollars," cried a voice out of the crowd. I thought I had heard the voice before, and looked up to see who had spoken. It was a tall man with haik over his turban, and blue selam on top of a yellow kaftan.

"A hundred dollars offered," cried the salesman, "only a hundred. Brothers, now's the chance for all true believers."

"A hundred and five," cried another voice.

"A hundred and ten."

"A hundred and fifteen."

"A hundred and fifteen for this jewel of a girl," cried the salesman. "It's giving her away, brothers. By the prophets, if you are not quick I'll keep her for myself. Come, look at her, Sidi. Isn't she good enough for a sultan? The Prophet (God rest him) would have leaped at her. He loved sweet women as much as he loved sweet odors. Now, for the third and last time—how much? Remember, I guarantee her seventeen years of age, sound, strong, plump, and sweet."

"A hundred and twenty," cried the voice I had heard first. I looked up at the speaker again. It was the American in his Moorish costume.

I could bear no more of the sickening spectacle, and as I turned aside with my interpreter, I was conscious that my companion of the voyage was following me. When we came to some dark arches that divided Old Fez from New Fez the American spoke, and I sent my interpreter ahead.

"You see I am giving myself full tether in this execrable land," he said.

"Indeed you are," I answered.

"Well, as the Romans in Rome, you know—it was what I came for," he said.

"Take care," I replied. "Take care."

He drew up shortly and said, "By the way, I ought to be ashamed to meet you."

I thought he ought, but for courtesy I asked him why.

"Because," he said, "I have failed to act up to my principles."

"In what?" I inquired.

"In saving the life of a scoundrel at the risk of my own," he answered.

Then he told me his story. "I left Tangier," he said, "with four men in my caravan, but it did not suit me to bring them into Fez, so I dismissed them a day's ride from here, paying in full for the whole journey and making a present over. My generosity was a blunder. The Moor can not comprehend an act of disinterested kindness, and I saw the ruffians lay their heads together to find out what it could mean. Three of them gave it up and went off home, but the fourth determined to follow the trace. His name was Larby."

Larby! El Arby, my son? Did you say El Arby? Of Tangier, too? A Moor? Or was he a Spanish renegade turned Muslim? But no matter—no matter.

"He was my guide," said the American, "and a most brazen hypocrite, always cheating me. I let him do so, it amused me—always lying to my face, and always fumbling his beads—'God forgive me! God forgive me'—an appropriate penance, you know the way of it. 'Peace, Sidi!' said the rascal: 'Farewell! Allah send we meet in Paradise.' But the devil meant that we should meet before that. We have met. It was a hot moment. Do you know the Hamadshá Mosque? It is a place in a side street sacred to the preaching of a fanatical follower of one Sidi Ali bin Hamdoosh, and to certain wild dances executed in a glass and fire eating frenzy. I thought I should like to hear a Moorish D. L. Moody, and one day I went there. As I was going in I met a man coming out. It was Larby. 'Beeba!' he whispered, with a tragic start—that was his own name for me on the journey. 'Keep your tongue between your teeth,' I whispered back. 'I was Beeba yesterday, to-day I'm Sidi Mohammed.' Then I entered, I spread my prayer-mat, chanted my first Sura, listened to a lusty sermon, and came out. There, as I expected, in the blind lane leading from the Hamadshá to the town was Larby waiting for me. 'Beeba,' said he, with a grin, 'you play a double hand of cards.' 'Then,' said I, 'take care I don't trump your trick.' The rascal had thought I might bribe him, and when he knew that I would not I saw murder in his face. He had conceived the idea of betraying me at the next opportunity. At that moment he was as surely aiming at my life as if he had drawn his dagger and stabbed me. It was then that I disgraced my principles."

"How? how?" I said, though truly I had little need to ask.

"We were alone, I tell you, in a blind lane," said the American; "but I remembered stories the man had told me of his children. 'Little Hoolia,' he called his daughter, a pretty, black-eyed mite of six, who always watched for him when he was away."

I was breaking into perspiration. "Do you mean," I said, "that you should have—"

"I mean that I should have killed the scoundrel there and then!" said the American.

"God forbid it!" I cried, and my hair rose from my scalp in horror.

"Why not?" said the American. "It would have been an act of *self-defense*. The man meant to kill me. He will kill me still if I give him the chance. What is the difference between murder in a moment and murder after five, ten, fifteen, twenty days? Only that one is murder in hot blood and haste and the other is murder in cold blood and by stealth. Is it life that you think so precious? Then why should I value *his* life more than I value *my own*?"

I shivered, and could say nothing.

"You think me a monster," said the American, "but remember, since we left England the atmosphere has changed."

"Remember, too," I said, "that this man can do you no harm unless you intrude yourself upon his superstitions again. Leave the country immediately; depend upon it, he is following you."

"That's not possible," said the American, "for *I* am following *him*. Until I come up with him I can do nothing, and my existence is not worth a pin's purchase."

I shuddered, and we parted. My mind told me that he was right, but my heart clamored above the voice of reason and said, "*You* could not do it, no, not to save a hundred lives."

Ah, father, how little we know ourselves—how little, oh, how little! When I think that *he* shrank back—he who held life so cheap—while *I*—I who held it so dear, so sacred, so god-like—Bear with me; I will tell all.

I met the American at intervals during the next six days. We did not often speak, but as we passed in the streets—he alone, I always with my loquacious interpreter—I observed with dread the change that the shadow of death hanging over a man's head can bring to pass in his face and manner. He grew thin and sallow and wild-eyed. One day he stopped me, and said: "I know now what your Buckshot Forster died of," and then he went on without another word.

But about ten days after our first meeting in the slave market he stopped me again, and said, quite cheerfully: "He has gone home—I'm satisfied of that now."

"Thank God!" I answered involuntarily.

"Ah," he said, with a twinkle of the eye, "who says that a man must hang up his humanity on the peg with his hat in the hospital hall when he goes to be a surgeon? If the poet Keats had got over the first shock to his sensibilities, he might have been the greatest surgeon of his day."

"You'll be more careful in future," I said, "not to cross the fanaticism of these fanatics?"

He smiled, and asked if I knew the Karueein Mosque. I told him I had seen it.

"It is the greatest in Morocco," he said. "The Moors say the inner court stands on eight hundred pillars. I don't believe them, and I mean to see for myself."

I found it useless to protest, and he went his way, laughing at my blanched and bewildered face. "That man," I thought, "is fit to be the hero of a tragedy, and he is wasting himself on a farce."

Meanwhile, I had a shadow over my own life which would not lift. That letter which I had received from home at the moment of leaving Tangier had haunted me throughout the journey. Its brevity, its insufficiency, its delay, and above all its conspicuous omission of all mention of our boy had given rise to endless speculation. Every dark possibility that fancy could devise had risen before me by way of explanation. I despised myself for such weakness, but self-contempt did nothing to allay my vague fears. The child was ill; I knew it; I felt it; I could swear to it as certainly as if my ears could hear the labored breathing in his throat.

Nevertheless I went on; so much did my philosophy do for me. But when I got to Fez I walked straightway to the English post-office to see if there was a letter awaiting me. Of course there was no letter there. I had not reflected that I had come direct from the port through which the mails had to pass, and that if the postal courier had gone by me on the road I must have seen him, which I had not.

I was ashamed before my own consciousness, but all the same the post-office saw me every day. Whatever the direction that I took with my interpreter, it led toward that destination in the end. And whatever the subject of his ceaseless gabble—a very deluge of words—it was forced to come round at last to the times and seasons of the mails from

England. These were bi-weekly, with various possibilities of casual arrivals besides.

Fez is a noble city, the largest and finest Oriental city I had yet seen, fit to compare in its own much different way of beauty and of splendor with the great cities of the West, the great cities of the earth, and of all time; but for me its attractions were overshadowed by the gloom of my anxiety. The atmosphere of an older world, the spirit of the East, the sense of being transported to Bible times, the startling interpretations which the Biblical stories were receiving by the events of every day—these brought me no pleasure. As for the constant reminders of the presence of Islam every hour, at every corner, the perpetual breath of prayer and praise, which filled this land that was corrupt to the core, they gave me pain more poignant than disgust. The call of the mueddin in the early morning was a daily agony. I slept three streets from the Karueein minarets, but the voice seemed to float into my room in the darkness, and coil round my head and ring in my ears. Always I was awakened at the first sound of the stentorian "Allah-u-Kabar," or, if I awoke in the silence and thought with a feeling of relief, "It is over, I have slept through it," the howling wail would suddenly break in upon my thanksgiving.

There was just one fact of life in Fez that gave me a kind of melancholy joy. At nearly every turn of a street my ears were arrested by the multitudinous cackle, the broken, various-voiced sing-song of a children's school. These Moorish schools interested me. They were the simplest of all possible institutes, consisting usually of a rush-covered cellar, two steps down from the street, with the teacher, the Táleb, often a half-blind old man, squatting in the middle of the floor, and his pupils seated about him, and all reciting together some passages of the Koran, the only textbook of education. One such school was close under my bedroom window; I heard the drone of it as early as seven o'clock every morning, and as often as I went abroad I stood for a moment and looked in at the open doorway. A black boy sat there with a basket for the alms of passers-by. He was a bright-eyed little fellow, six or seven years of age, and he knew one English phrase only: "Come on," he would say, and hold up the basket and smile. What pathetic interest his sunny face had for me, how he would cheer and touch me, with what strange memories his voice and laugh would startle me, it would be pitiful to tell.

Bear with me! I was far from my own darling, I was in a strange land, I was a weak man for all that I was thought so strong, and my one besetting infirmity—more consuming than a mother's love—was preyed upon by my failing health, which in turn was preying upon it.

And if the sights of the streets brought me pain, or pleasure that was akin to pain, what of the sights, the visions, the dreams of my own solitary mind! I could not close my eyes in the darkness but I saw my boy. His little child-ghost was always with me. He never appeared as I had oftenest seen him—laughing, romping, and kicking up his legs on the hearth-rug. Sometimes he came as he would do at home after he committed some childish trespass and I had whipped him—opening the door of my room and stepping one pace in, quietly, nervously, half fearfully, to say good-night and kiss me at his bedtime, and I would lift my eyes and see, over the shade of my library lamp, his little sober red-and-white face just dried of its recent tears. Or, again, sometimes I myself would seem in these dumb dramas of the darkness to go into his room when he was asleep, that I might indulge my hungry foolish heart with looks of fondness that the reproving parent could not give, and find him sleeping with an open book in his hands, which he had made believe to read. And then for sheer folly of love I would pick up his wee knickerbockers and turn out its load at either side, to see what a boy's pockets might be like, and discover a curiosity shop of poor little treasures—a knife with a broken blade, a nail, two marbles, a bit of brass, some string, a screw, a crust of bread, a cork, and a leg of a lobster.

While I was indulging this weakness the conviction was deepening in my mind that my boy was ill. So strong did this assurance become at length, that, though I was ashamed to give way to it so far as to set my face toward home, being yet no better for my holiday, I sat down at length to write a letter to Wenman—I had written to my wife by every mail—that I might relieve my pent-up feelings. I said nothing to him of my misgivings, for I was loth to confess to them, having no positive reasons whatever, and no negative grounds except the fact that I was receiving no letters. But I gave him a full history of my boy's case, described each stage of it in the past, foretold its probable developments in the future, indicated with elaborate care the treatment necessary at every point, and foreshadowed the contingencies under which it might in the end become malignant and even deadly unless stopped by the operation that I had myself, after years of labor, found the art of making.

I spent an afternoon in the writing of this letter, and when it was done I felt as if a burden that had been on my back for ages had suddenly been lifted away. Then I went out alone to post it. The time was close to evening prayers, and as I walked through the streets the Tálebs and tradesmen, with their prayer-mats under their arms, were trooping into the various mosques. Going by the Karueein Mosque I observed that the Good Muslimeen were entering it by hundreds. "Some special celebration," I thought. My heart was light, my eyes were alert, and my step was quick. For the first time since my coming to the city, Fez seemed to me a beautiful place. The witchery of the scenes of the streets took hold of me. To be thus transported into a world of two thousand years ago gave me the delight of magic.

When I reached the English post-office I found it shut up. On its shutters behind its iron grating a notice-board was hung out, saying that the office was temporarily closed for the sorting of an incoming mail and the despatch of an outgoing one. There was a little crowd of people waiting in front—chiefly Moorish servants of English visitors— for the window to open again, and near by stood the horses of the postal couriers pawing the pavement. I dropped my letter into the slit in the window, and then stood aside to see if the mail had brought anything for me at last.

The window was thrown up, and two letters were handed to me through the grating over the heads of the Moors, who were crushing underneath. I took them with a sort of fear, and half wished at the first moment that they might be from strangers. They were from home; one was from my wife—I knew the envelope before looking at the handwriting—the other was from Wenman.

I read Wenman's letter first. Good or bad, the news must be broken to me gently. Hardly had I torn the sheet open when I saw what it contained. My little Noel had been ill; he was still so, but not seriously, and I was not to be alarmed. The silence on their part which I had complained of so bitterly had merely been due to their fear of giving me unnecessary anxiety. For his part (Wenman's) he would have written before, relying on my manliness and good sense, but my wife had restrained him, saying she knew me better. There was no cause for apprehension; the boy was going along as well as could be expected, etc., etc., etc., etc.

Not a word to indicate the nature and degree of the attack. Such an insufficient epistle must have disquieted the veriest nincompoop alive. To send a thing like that to *me*—to me of all men! Was there ever so gross a mistake of judgment?

I knew in an instant what the fact must be—my boy was down with that old congenital infirmity of the throat. Surely my wife had told me more. She had. Not by design, but unwittingly she had revealed the truth to me. Granville Wenman had written to me, she said, explaining everything, and I was not to worry and bother. All that was possible was being done for our darling, and if I were there I could do no more. The illness had to have its course, so I must be patient. All this is the usual jargon of the surgery—I knew that Wenman had dictated it—and then a true line or two worth all the rest from my dear girl's own bleeding mother's heart. Our poor Noel was this, and that, he complained of so-and-so, and first began to look unwell in such and such ways.

It was clear as noonday. The attack of the throat which I had foreseen had come. Five years I had looked for it. Through five long years I had waited and watched to check it. I had labored day and night that when it should come I might meet it. My own health I had wasted—and for what? For fame, for wealth, for humanity, for science? No, no, no, but for the life of my boy. And now when his enemy was upon him at length, where was I—I who alone in all this world of God could save him? I was thirteen hundred miles from home.

Oh, the irony of my fate! My soul rose in rebellion against it. Staggering back through the darkening streets, the whole city seemed dead and damned.

How far I walked in this state of oblivion I do not know, but presently out of the vague atmosphere wherein all things had been effaced I became conscious, like one awakening after a drug, of an unusual commotion going on around. People were running past me and across me in the direction of the Karueein Mosque. From that place a loud tumult was rising into the air. The noise was increasing with every moment, and rising to a Babel of human voices.

I did not very much heed the commotion. What were the paltry excitements of life to me now? I was repeating to myself the last words of my poor wife's letter: "How I miss you, and wish you were with me!" "I will go back," I was telling myself, "I will go back."

In the confusion of my mind I heard snatches of words spoken by the people as they ran by me. "Nazarene!" "Christian!" "Cursed Jew!" These were hissed out at each other by the Moors as they were scurrying past. At length I heard a Spaniard shout up to a fellow-countryman who was on a house-top: "Englishman caught in the mosque."

At that my disordered senses recovered themselves, and suddenly I became aware that the tumult was coming in my direction. The noise grew deeper, louder, and more shrill at every step. In another moment it had burst upon me in a whirlpool of uproar.

Round the corner of the narrow lane that led to the Karueein Mosque a crowd of people came roaring like a torrent. They were Moors, Arabs, and Berbers, and they were shouting, shrieking, yelling, and uttering every sound that the human voice can make. At the first instant I realized no more than this, but at the next I saw that the people were hunting a man as hounds hunt a wolf. The man was flying before them; he was coming toward me: in the gathering darkness I could see him; his dress, which was Moorish, was torn into shreds about his body; his head was bare; his chest was bleeding; I saw his face—it was the face of the American, my companion of the voyage.

He saw me too, and at that instant he turned about and faced full upon his pursuers. What happened then I dare not tell.

Father, he was a brave man, and he sold his life dearly. But he fell at last. He was but one to a hundred. The yelping human dogs trod him down like vermin.

I am a coward. I fled and left him. When I got back to my lodgings I called for my guide, for I was resolved to leave Fez without an hour's delay. The guide was not to be found, and I had to go in search of him. When I lighted on him, at length, he was in a dingy coffee-house, squatting on the ground by the side of another Moor, an evil-looking scoundrel, who was reciting some brave adventure to a group of admiring listeners.

I called my man out and told him of my purpose. He lifted his hands in consternation. "Leave Fez to-night?" he said. "Impossible, my sultan, impossible! My lord has not heard the order!"

"What order?" I asked. I was alarmed. Must I be a prisoner in Morocco while my child lay dying in England?

"That the gates be closed and no Christian allowed to leave the city until the morning. It is the order of the Kaleefa, my sultan, since the outrage of the Christian in the mosque this morning."

I suspected the meaning of this move in an instant, and the guide's answer to my questions ratified my fears. One man, out of madness or thirst for revenge, had led the attack upon the American, and a crowd of fanatics had killed him—giving him no chance of retreat with his life, either by circumcision or the profession of Islam. But cooler heads had already found time to think of the penalty of shedding Christian blood. That penalty was twofold: first, the penalty of disgrace which would come of the idea that the lives of Christians were not safe in Morocco, and next, the penalty of hard dollars to be paid to the American Minister at Tangier.

To escape from the double danger the outrage was to be hushed up. Circumstances lent themselves to this artifice. True, that passage of the American across country had been known in every village through which he had passed; but at the gates of Fez he had himself cut off all trace of his identity. He had entered the city alone, or in disguise. His arrival as a stranger had not been notified at any of the "clubs" or bazaars. Only one man had recognized him: that man was Larby, his guide.

The body was to be buried secretly, no Christian being allowed to see it. Then the report was to be given out that the dead man had been a Moorish subject, that he had been killed in a blood-fued, and that the rumor that he was a Christian caught in the act of defying the mosque was an error, without the shadow of truth in it. But until all this had been done no Christian should be allowed to pass through the gates. As things stood at present the first impulse of a European would be to fly to the Consul with the dangerous news.

I knew something of the Moors and their country by this time, and I left Fez that night, but it cost me fifty pounds to get out of it. There was a bribe for the kaid, a bribe for the Kaleefa, and bribes for every ragged Jack of the underlings down to the porter at the gate.

With all my horror and the fever of my anxiety, I could have laughed in the face of the first of these functionaries. Between his greedy desire of the present I was offering him, his suspicion that I knew something of the identity of the Christian who had been killed, his misgivings as to the reasons of my sudden flight, and his dread that I would discover the circumstances of the American's death, the figure he cut was a foolish one. But why should I reproach the man's duplicity? I was practising the like of it myself. Too well I knew that if I betrayed any knowledge of what had happened it would be impossible that I should be allowed to leave Fez.

So I pretended to know nothing. It was a ridiculous interview.

On my way back from it I crossed a little company of Moors, leading, surrounding, and following a donkey. The donkey was heavily laden with what appeared to be two great panniers of rubbish. It was dusk, but my sight has always been keen, and I could not help seeing that hidden under the rubbish there was another burden on the donkey's back. It was the body of a dead man. I had little doubt of who the dead man must be; but I hastened on and did not look again. The Moors turned into a garden as I passed them. I guessed what they were about to do there, but my own danger threatened me, and I wished to see and know no more.

As I was passing out of the town in the moonlight an hour before midnight, with my grumbling tentmen and muleteers at my heels, a man stepped out of the shadow of the gateway arch and leered in my face, and said in broken English, "So your Christian friend is corrected by Allah!"

Moorish English, my son, or Spanish?

Spanish.

It was the scoundrel whom I had seen in the coffee-house. I knew he must be Larby, and that he had betrayed his master at last. Also, I knew that he was aware that I had seen all. At that moment, looking down from my horse's back into the man's evil face my whole nature changed. I remembered the one opportunity which the American had lost out of a wandering impulse of human tenderness—of saving his own life by taking the life of him that threatened it, and I said in my heart of hearts, "Now God in heaven keep me from the like temptation."

Ah! father, do not shrink from me; think of it, only think of it! I was fifteen hundred miles from home, and I was going back to my dying boy.

God keep you, indeed, my son. Your feet were set in a slippery place. El Arby, you say? A man of your own age? Dark? Sallow? It must be the same. Long ago I knew the man you speak of. It was under another name, and in another country. Yes, he was all you say. God forgive him, God forgive him! Poor wrecked and bankrupt soul. His evil angel was always at his hand, and his good one far away. He brought his father to shame, and his mother to the grave. There was a crime and conviction, then banishment, and after that his father fled from the world. But the Church is peace; he took refuge with her, and all is well. Go on now.

III

F ather, I counted it up. Every mile of the distance I counted it. And I reckoned every hour since my wife's letter had been written against the progress and period of my boy's disease. So many days since the date of the letter, and Noel had been ailing and ill so many days before that. The gross sum of those days was so much, and in that time the affection, if it ran the course I looked for, must have reached such and such a stage. While I toiled along over the broad wastes of that desolate land, I seemed to know at any moment what the condition must be at the utmost and best of my boy in his bed at home.

Then I reckoned the future as well as the past. So many days it would take me to ride to Tangier, so many hours to cross from Tangier to Cadiz, so many days and nights by rail from Cadiz to London. The grand total of time past since my poor Noel first became unwell, and of time to come before I could reach his side, would be so much. What would his condition be then? I knew that also. It would be so and so.

Thus, step by step I counted it all up. The interval would be long, very long, between the beginning of the attack and my getting home, but not too long for my hopes. All going well with me, I should still arrive in time. If the disease had taken an evil turn, my boy might perhaps be in its last stages. But then *I* would be there, and I could save him. The operation which I had spent five years of my life to master would bring him back from the gates of death itself.

Father, I had no doubt of that, and I had no doubt of my calculations. Lying here now it seems as if the fiends themselves must have shrieked to see me in that far-off land gambling like a fool in the certainty of the life I loved, and reckoning nothing of the hundred poor chances that might snuff it out like a candle. Call it frenzy, call it madness, nevertheless it kept my heart alive, and saved me from despair.

But, oh! the agony of my impatience! If anything should stop me now! Let me be one day later—only one—and what might not occur! Then, how many were the dangers of delay! First, there was the possibility of illness overtaking me. My health was not better, but worse, than when I left home. I was riding from sunrise to sunset, and not sleeping at nights. No matter! I put all fear from that cause away from me. Though my limbs refused to bear me up, and under the affliction of my nerves my muscles lost the power to hold the reins, yet if I could be slung on to the back of my horse I should still go on.

But then there was the worse danger of coming into collision with the fanaticism of the people through whose country I had to pass. I did not fear the fate of the American, for I could not be guilty of his folly. But I remembered the admission of the English Consul at Tangier that a stranger might offend the superstitions of the Moslems unwittingly; I recalled his parting words of counsel, spoken half in jest, "Keep out of a Moorish prison"; and the noisome dungeon into which the young Berber had been cast arose before my mind in visions of horror.

What precautions I took to avoid these dangers of delay would be a long and foolish story. Also, it would be a mean and abject one, and I should be ashamed to tell it. How I saluted every scurvy beggar on the way with the salutation of his faith and country; how I dismounted as I approached a town or a village, and only returned to the saddle when I had gone through it: how I uncovered my head—in ignorance of Eastern custom—as I went by a saint's house, and how at length (remembering the Jewish banker who was beaten) I took off my shoes and walked barefoot as I passed in front of a mosque.

Yes, it was I who paid all this needless homage; I whose pride has always been my bane; I who could not bend the knee to be made a knight; I who had felt humility before no man. Even so it was. In my eagerness, my impatience, my dread of impediment on my journey home to my darling who waited for me there, I was studying the faces and groveling at the feet of that race of ignorant fanatics.

But the worst of my impediments were within my own camp. The American was right. The Moor can not comprehend a disinterested action. My foolish homage to their faith awakened the suspicions of my men. When they had tried in vain to fathom the meaning of it, they agreed to despise me. I did not heed their contempt, but I was compelled to take note of its consequences. From being my servants, they became my masters. When it pleased them to encamp I had to rest, though my inclination was to go on, and only when it suited them to set out again could I resume my journey. In vain did I protest, and plead, and threaten. The Moor is often a brave man, but these men were a gang of white-livered poltroons, and a blow would have served to subdue them. With visions of a Moorish prison before my eyes I dared not raise my hand. One weapon alone could I, in my own cowardice, employ against them—bribes, bribes, bribes. Such was the sole instrument with which I combated their laziness, their duplicity, and their deceit.

Father, I was a pitiful sight in my weakness and my impatience. We had not gone far out of Fez when I observed that the man Larby was at the heels of our company. This alarmed me, and I called to my guide.

"Alee," I said, "who is that evil-looking fellow?"

Alee threw up both hands in amazement. "Evil-looking fellow!" he cried. "God be gracious to my father! Who does my lord mean? Not Larby; no, not Larby. Larby is a good man. He lives in one of the mosque houses at Tangier. The Nadir leased it to him, and he keeps his shop on the Sôk de Barra. Allah bless Larby. Should you want musk, should you want cinnamon, Larby is the man to sell to you. But sometimes he guides Christians to Fez, and then his brother keeps his shop for him."

"But why is the man following us?" I asked.

"My sultan," said Alee, "am I not telling you? Larby is returning home. The Christian he took to Fez, where is he?"

"Yes," I said, "where is he?"

Alee grinned, and answered: "He is gone—southward, my lord."

"Why should you lie to me like that?" I said. "You know the Christian is dead, and that this Larby was the means of killing him!"

"Shoo! What is my lord saying?" cried Alee, lifting his fat hands with a warning gesture. "What did my lord tell the Basha? My lord must know nothing—nothing. It would not be safe."

Then with glances of fear toward Larby, and dropping his voice to a whisper, Alee added, "It is true the Christian is dead; he died last sunset. Allah corrected him. So Larby is going back alone, going back to his shop, to his house, to his wives, to his little daughter Hoolia. Allah send Larby a safe return. Not following us, Sidi. No, no; Larby is going back the same way—that is all."

The answer did not content me, but I could say no more. Nevertheless, my uneasiness at the man's presence increased hour by hour. I could not think of him without thinking also of the American and of the scene of horror near to the Karueein Mosque. I could not look at him but the blood down my back ran cold. So I called my guide again, and said, "Send that man away; I will not have him in our company."

Alee pretended to be deeply wounded. "Sidi," he said, "ask anything else of me. What will you ask? Will you ask me to die for you? I am ready, I am willing, I am satisfied. But Larby is my friend. Larby is my brother, and this thing you ask of me I can not do. Allah has not written it. Sidi, it can not be."

With such protestations—the common cant of the country—I had need to be content. But now the impression fixed itself upon my mind that the evil-faced scoundrel who had betrayed the American to his death was not only following *us* but *me*. Oh! the torment of that idea in the impatience of my spirit and the racking fever of my nerves! To be dogged day and night as by a bloodhound, never to raise my eyes without the dread of encountering the man's watchful eye—the agony of the incubus was unbearable!

My first thought was merely that the rascal meant robbery. However far I might ride ahead of my own people in the daytime he was always close behind me, and as surely as I wandered away from the camp at nightfall I was overtaken by him or else I met him face to face.

"Alee," I said at last, "that man is a thief."

Of course Alee was horrified. "Ya Allah!" he cried. "What is my lord saying? The Moor is no thief. The Moor is true, the Moor is honest. None so true and honest as the Moor. Wherefore should the Moor be a thief? To be a thief in Barbary is to be a fool. Say I rob a Christian. Good. I kill him and take all he has and bury him in a lonely place. All right. What happens? Behold, Sidi, this is what happens. Your Christian Consul says, 'Where is the Christian you took to Fez?' I can not tell. I lie, I deceive, I make excuses. No use. Your Christian Consul goes to the Kasbah, and says to the Basha: 'Cast that Moor into prison, he is a robber and a murderer!' Then he goes to the Sultan at Marrakesh, in the name of your Queen, who lives in the country of the Nazarenes, over the sea. 'Pay me twenty thousand dollars,' he says, 'for the life of my Christian who is robbed and murdered,' Just so. The Sultan—Allah preserve our Mulai Hassan!—he pays the dollars. Good, all right, just so. But is that all, Sidi? No, Sidi, that is not all. The Sultan—God prolong the life of our merciful lord—he then comes to my people, to my Basha, to my bashalic, and he says, 'Pay me back my forty thousand dollars'—do you hear me, Sidi, *forty* thousand!—'for the Nazarene who is dead.' All right. But we can not pay. Good. The Sultan—Allah save him!—he comes, he takes all we have, he puts every man of my people to the sword. We are gone, we are wiped out. Did I not say, Sidi, to be a thief in Barbary is to be a fool?"

It was cold comfort. That the man Larby was following me I was confident, and that he meant to rob me I was at first convinced. Small solace, therefore, in the thought that if the worst befell me, and my boy at home died for want of his father, who lay robbed and murdered in those desolate wastes, my Government would exact a claim in paltry dollars.

My next thought was that the man was merely watching me out of the country. That he was aware that I knew his secret was only too certain; that he had betrayed my knowledge to the authorities at the capital after I had parted from them was more than probable, and it was not impossible that the very men who had taken bribes of me had in their turn bribed him that he might follow me and see that I did not inform the Ministers and Consuls of foreign countries of the murder of the American in the streets of Fez.

That theory partly reconciled me to the man's presence: Let him watch. His constant company was in its tormenting way my best security. I should go to no Minister, and no Consul should see me. I had too much reason to think of my own living affairs to busy myself with those of the dead American.

But such poor unction as this reflection brought me was dissipated by a second thought. What security for the man himself, or for the authorities who might have bribed him—or perhaps menaced him—to watch me would lie in the fact that I had passed out of the country without revealing the facts of the crime which I had witnessed? Safely back in England, I might tell all with safety. Once let me leave Morocco with their secret in my breast, and both the penalties these people dreaded might be upon them. Merely to watch me was wasted labor. They meant to do more, or they would have done nothing.

Thinking so, another idea took possession of me with a shock of terror—the man was following me to kill me as the sole Christian witness of the crime that had been committed. By the light of that theory everything became plain. When I visited the Kasbah nothing was known of my acquaintance with the murdered man. My bribes were taken, and I was allowed to leave Fez in spite of public orders. But then came Larby with alarming intelligence. I had been a friend of the American, and had been seen to speak with him in the public streets. Perhaps Larby himself had seen me, or perhaps my own guide, Alee, had betrayed me to his friend and "brother." At that the Kaid or his Kaleefa had raised their eyebrows and sworn at each other for simpletons and fools. To think that the very man who had intended to betray them had come with an innocent face and a tale of a sick child in England! To think that they had suffered him to slip through their fingers and leave them some paltry bribes of fifty pounds! Fifty pounds taken by stealth against twenty thousand dollars to be plumped down after the Christian had told his story! These Nazarenes were so subtle, and the sons of Ishmael were so simple. But diamond cut diamond. Everything was not lost. One hundred and twenty-five miles this Christian had still to travel before he could sail from Barbary, and not another Christian could he encounter on that journey. Then up, Larby, and after him! God make your way easy! Remember, Larby, remember, good fellow, it is not only the pockets of the people of Fez that are in danger if that Christian should escape. Let him leave the Gharb alive, and your own neck is in peril. You were the spy, you were the informer, you were the hotheaded madman who led the attack that ended in the spilling of Christian blood. If the Sultan should have to pay twenty thousand dollars to the Minister for America at Tangier for the life of this dead dog whom we have grubbed into the earth in a garden, if the Basha of Fez should have to pay forty thousand dollars to the Sultan, if the people should have to pay eighty thousand dollars to the Basha, then you, Larby, you in your turn will have to pay with your *life* to the people. It is *your* life against the life of the Christian. So follow him, watch him, silence him, he knows your secret—away!

Such was my notion of what happened at the Kasbah of Fez after I had passed the gates of the city. It was a wild vision, but to my distempered imagination it seemed to be a plausible theory. And now Larby, the spy upon the American, Larby, my assassin-elect, Larby, who to save his own life must take mine, Larby was with me, was beside me, was behind me constantly!

God help you, my son, God help you! Larby! O Larby! Again, again!

What was I to do? Open my heart to Larby; to tell him it was a blunder; that I meant no man mischief; that I was merely hastening back to my sick boy, who was dying for want of me? That was impossible; Larby would laugh in my face, and still follow me. Bribe him? That was useless; Larby would take my money and make the surer of his victim. It was a difficult problem; but at length I hit on a solution. Father, you will pity me for a fool when you hear it. I would bargain with Larby as Faust bargained with the devil. He should give me two weeks of life, and come with me to England. I should do my work here, and Larby should never leave my side. My boy's life should be saved by that operation, which I alone knew how to perform. After that Larby and I should square accounts together. He should have all the money I had in the world, and the passport of my name and influence for his return to his own country. I should write a confession of suicide, and then—and then—only then—at home—here in my own room—Larby should kill me in order to satisfy himself that his own secret and the secret of his people must be safe forever.

It was a mad dream, but what dream of dear life is not mad that comes to the man whom death dogs like a bloodhound? And mad as it was I tried to make it come true. The man was constantly near me, and on the third morning of our journey I drew up sharply, and said:

"Larby!"

"Sidi," he answered.

"Would you not like to go on with me to England?"

He looked at me with his glittering eyes, and I gave an involuntary shiver. I had awakened the man's suspicions in an instant. He thought I meant to entrap him. But he only smiled knowingly, shrugged his shoulders, and answered civilly: "I have my shop in the Sôk de Barra, Sidi. And then there are my wives and my sons and my little Hoolia— God be praised for all his blessings."

"Hoolia?" I asked.

"My little daughter, Sidi."

"How old is she?"

"Six, Sidi, only six, but as fair as an angel."

"I dare say she misses you when you are away, Larby," I said.

"You have truth, Sidi. She sits in the Sôk by the tents of the brassworkers and plaits rushes all the day long, and looks over to where the camels come by the saints' houses on the hill, and waits and watches."

"Larby," I said, "I, too, have a child at home who is waiting and watching. A boy, my little Noel, six years of age, just as old as your own little Hoolia. And so bright, so winsome. But he is ill, he is dying, and he is all the world to me. Larby, I am a surgeon, I am a doctor, if I could but reach England—"

It was worse than useless. I stopped, for I could go no farther. The cold glitter of the man's eyes passed over me like frost over flame, and I knew his thought as well as if he had spoken it. "I have heard that story before," he was telling himself, "I have heard it at the Kasbah, and it is a lie and a trick."

My plan was folly, and I abandoned it; but I was more than ever convinced of my theory. This man was following me to kill me. He was waiting an opportunity to do his work safely, secretly, and effectually. His rulers would shield him in his crime, for by that crime they would themselves be shielded.

Father, my theory, like my plan, was foolishness. Only a madman would have dreamt of concealing a crime whereof there was but one witness, by a second crime, whereof the witnesses must have been five hundred. The American had traveled in disguise and cut off the trace of his identity to all men save myself. When he died at the hands of the fanatics whose faith he had outraged, I alone of all Christians knew that it was Christian blood that had stained the streets of Fez. But how different my own death must have been. I had traveled openly as a Christian and an Englishman. At the consulate of Tangier I was known by name and repute, and at that of Fez I had registered myself. My presence had been notified at every town I had passed through, and the men of my caravan would not have dared to return to their homes without me. In the case of the murder of the American the chances to the Moorish authorities of claim for indemnity were as one to five hundred. In the case of the like catastrophe to myself they must have been as five hundred to one. Thus, in spite of fanaticism and the ineradicable hatred of the Moslem for the Nazarene, Morocco to me, as to all Christian travelers, traveling openly and behaving themselves properly, was as safe a place as England itself.

But how can a man be hot and cold and wise and foolish in a moment? I was in no humor to put the matter to myself temperately, and, though I had been so cool as to persuade myself that the authorities whom I had bribed could not have been madmen enough to think that they could conceal the murder of the American by murdering me, yet I must have remained convinced that Larby himself was such a madman.

As a surgeon, I had some knowledge of madness, and the cold, clear, steely glitter of the man's eyes when he looked at me was a thing that I could not mistake. I had seen it before in religious monomaniacs. It was an infallible and fatal sign. With that light in the eyes, like the glance of a dagger, men will kill the wives they love, and women will slaughter the children of their bosom. When I saw it in Larby I shivered with a chilly presentiment. It seemed to say that I should see my home no more. I have seen my home once more; I am back in England, I am here, but—

No, no, not That! *Larby! Don't tell* Me *you did* That.

Father, is my crime so dark? That hour comes back and back. How long will it haunt me? How long? For ever and ever. When time for me is swallowed up in eternity, eternity will be swallowed up in the memory of that hour. Peace! Do you say peace? Ah! yes, yes; God is merciful!

Before I had spoken to Larby his presence in our company had been only as a dark and fateful shadow. Now it was a foul and hateful incubus. Never in all my life until then had I felt hatred for any human creature. But I hated that man with all the sinews of my soul. What was it to me that he was a madman? He intended to keep me from my dying boy. Why should I feel tenderness toward him because he was the father of his little Hoolia? By killing me he would kill my little Noel.

I began to recall the doctrines of the American as he propounded them on the ship. It was the life of an honest man against the life of a scoundrel. These things should be rated *ad valorem*. If the worst came to the worst, why should I have more respect for this madman's life than for my own?

I looked at the man and measured his strength against mine. He was a brawny fellow with broad shoulders, and I was no better than a weakling. I was afraid of him, but I was yet more afraid of myself. Sometimes I surprised my half-conscious mind in the act of taking out of its silver-mounted sheath the large curved knife which I had bought of the hawker at Tangier, and now wore in the belt of my Norfolk jacket. In my cowardice and my weakness this terrified me. Not all my borrowed philosophy served to support me against the fear of my own impulses. Meantime, I was in an agony of suspense and dread. The nights brought me no rest and the mornings no freshness.

On the fourth day out of Fez we arrived at Wazzan, and there, though the hour was still early, my men decided to encamp for the night. I protested, and they retorted; I threatened, and they excused themselves. The mules wanted shoeing. I offered to pay double that they might be shod immediately. The tents were torn by a heavy wind the previous night. I offered to buy new ones. When their trumpery excuses failed them, the men rebelled openly, and declared their determination not to stir out of Wazzan that night.

But they had reckoned without their host this time. I found that there was an English Consul at Wazzan, and I went in search of him. His name was Smith, and he was a typical Englishman—ample, expansive, firm, resolute, domineering, and not troubled with too much sentiment. I told him of the revolt of my people and of the tyranny of the subterfuges whereby they had repeatedly extorted bribes. The good fellow came to my relief. He was a man of purpose, and he had no dying child twelve hundred miles away to make him a fool and a coward.

"Men," he said, "you've got to start away with this gentleman at sundown, and ride night and day—do you hear me, night and day—until you come to Tangier. A servant of my own shall go with you, and if you stop or delay or halt or go slowly he shall see that every man of you is clapped into the Kasbah as a blackmailer and a thief."

There was no more talk of rebellion. The men protested that they had always been willing to travel. Sidi had been good to them, and they would be good to Sidi. At sundown they would be ready.

"You will have no more trouble, sir," said the Consul; "but I will come back to see you start."

I thanked him and we parted. It was still an hour before sunset, and I turned aside to look at the town. I had barely walked a dozen paces when I came face to face with Larby. In the turmoil of my conflict with the men I had actually forgotten him for one long hour. He looked at me with his glittering eyes, and then his cold, clear gaze followed the Consul as he passed down the street. That double glance was like a shadowy warning. It gave me a shock of terror.

How had I forgotten my resolve to baffle suspicion by exchanging no word or look with any European Minister or Consul as long as I remained in Morocco? The expression in the man's face was not to be mistaken. It seemed to say, "So you have told all; very well, Sidi, we shall see."

With a sense as of creeping and cringing I passed on. The shadow of death seemed to have fallen upon me at last. I felt myself to be a doomed man. That madman would surely kill me. He would watch his chance; I should never escape him; my home would see me no more; my boy would die for want of me.

A tingling noise, as of the jangling of bells, was in my ears. Perhaps it was the tinkling of the bells of the water-carriers, prolonged and unbroken. A gauzy mist danced before my eyes. Perhaps it was the palpitating haze which the sun cast back from the gilded domes and minarets.

Domes and minarets were everywhere in this town of Wazzan. It seemed to be a place of mosques and saints' houses. Where the wide arch and the trough of the mosque were not, there was the open door in the low white-washed wall of the saint's house, surmounted by its white flag. In my dazed condition, I was sometimes in danger of stumbling into such places unawares. At the instant of recovered consciousness I always remembered the warnings of my guide as I stood by the house of Sidi Gali at Tangier: "Sacred place? Yes, sacred. No Nazarene may enter it. But Moslems, yes, Moslems may fly here for sanctuary. Life to the Moslem, death to the Nazarene. So it is."

Oh, it is an awful thing to feel that death is waiting for you constantly, that at any moment, at any turn, at any corner it may be upon you! Such was my state as I walked on that evening, waiting for the sunset, through the streets of Wazzan. At one moment I was conscious of a sound in my ears above the din of traffic—the *Arrah* of the ass-drivers, the *Bálak* of the men riding mules, and the general clamor of tongues. It was the steady beat of a footstep close behind me. I knew whose footstep it was. I turned about quickly, and Larby was again face to face with me. He met my gaze with the same cold, glittering look. My impulse was to fly at his throat, but that I dare not do. I knew myself to be a coward, and I remembered the Moorish prison.

"Larby," I said, "what do you want?"

"Nothing, Sidi, nothing," he answered.

"Then why are you following me like this?"

"Following you, Sidi?" The fellow raised his eyebrows and lifted both hands in astonishment.

"Yes, following me, dogging me, watching me, tracking me down. What does it mean? Speak out plainly."

"Sidi is jesting," he said, with a mischievous smile. "Is not this Wazzan—the holy city of Wazzan? Sidi is looking at the streets, at the mosques, at the saints' houses. So is Larby. That is all."

One glance at the man's evil eyes would have told you that he lied.

"Which way are you going?" I asked.

"This way." With a motion of the head he indicated the street before him.

"Then I am going to this," I said, and I walked away in the opposite direction.

I resolved to return to the English Consul, to tell him everything, and claim his protection. Though all the Moorish authorities in Morocco were in league with this religious monomaniac, yet surely there was life and safety under English power for one whose only offense was that of being witness to a crime which might lead to a claim for indemnity.

That it should come to this, and I of all men should hear it! God help me! God lead me! God give me light! Light, light, O God; give me light!

IV

Full of this new purpose and of the vague hope inspired by it, I was making my way back to the house of the Consul, when I came upon two postal couriers newly arrived from Tangier on their way to Fez. They were drawn up, amid a throng of the townspeople, before the palace of the Grand Shereef, and with the Moorish passion for "powder-play" they were firing their matchlocks into the air as salute and signal. Sight of the mail-bags slung at their sides, and of the Shereef's satchel, which they had come some miles out of their course to deliver, suggested the thought that they might be carrying letters for me, which could never come to my hands unless they were given to me now. The couriers spoke some little English. I explained my case to them, and begged them to open their bags and see if anything had been sent forward in my name from Tangier to Fez. True to the phlegmatic character of the Moor in all affairs of common life, they protested that they dare not do so; the bags were tied and sealed, and none dare open them. If there were letters of mine inside they must go on to Fez, and then return to Tangier. But with the usual results I had recourse to my old expedient; a bribe broke the seals, the bags were searched and two letters were found for me.

The letters, like those that came to Fez, were one from my wife and one from Wenman. I could not wait till I was alone, but broke open the envelopes and read my letters where I stood. A little crowd of Moors had gathered about me—men, youths, boys, and children—the ragged inhabitants of the streets of the holy city. They seemed to be chaffing and laughing at my expense, but I paid no heed to them.

Just as before, so now, and for the same reason I read Wenman's letter first. I remember every word of it, for every word seemed to burn into my brain like flame.

"My dear fellow," wrote Wenman, "I think it my duty to tell you that your little son is seriously ill."

I knew it—I knew it; who knew it so well as I, though I was more than a thousand miles away?

"It is a strange fact that he is down with the very disease of the throat which you have for so long a time made your especial study. Such, at least, is our diagnosis, assisted by your own discoveries. The case has now reached that stage where we must contemplate the possibility of the operation which you have performed with such amazing results. Our only uneasiness arises from the circumstance that this operation has hitherto been done by no one except yourself. We have, however, your explanations and your diagrams, and on these we must rely. And, even if you were here, his is not a case in which your own hand should be engaged. Therefore, rest assured, my dear fellow," etc., etc.

Blockheads! If they had not done it already they must not do it at all. I would telegraph from Tangier that I was coming. Not a case for my hand! Fools, fools! It was a case for my hand only.

I did not stop to read the friendly part of Wenman's letter, the good soul's expression of sympathy and solicitude, but in the fever of my impatience, sweating at every pore and breaking into loud exclamations, I tore open the letter from my wife. My eyes swam over the sheet, and I missed much at that first reading, but the essential part of the message stood out before me as if written in red:

"We. . . so delighted. . . your letters. . . Glad you are having warm, beautiful weather. . . Trust. . . make you strong and well. . . We are having blizzards here. . . snowing to-day. . . I am sorry to tell you, dearest, that our darling is very ill. It is his throat again. This is Friday, and he has grown worse every day since I wrote on Monday. When he can speak he is always calling for you. He thinks if you were here he would soon be well. He is very weak, for he can take no nourishment, and he has grown so thin, poor little fellow. But he looks very lovely, and every night he says in his prayers, 'God bless papa, and bring him safely home'. . ."

I could bear no more, the page in my hands was blotted out, and for the first time since I became a man I broke into a flood of tears.

O Omnipotent Lord of Heaven and earth, to think that this child is as life of my life and soul of my soul, that he is dying, that I alone of all men living can save him, and that we are twelve hundred miles apart! Wipe them out, O Lord—wipe out this accursed space dividing us; annihilate it. Thou canst do all, thou canst remove mountains, and this is but a little thing to Thee. Give me my darling under my hands, and I will snatch him out of the arms of death itself.

Did I utter such words aloud out of the great tempest of my trouble? I can not say; I do not know. Only when I had lifted my eyes from my wife's letter did I become conscious of where I was and what was going on around me. I was still in the midst of the crowd of idlers, and they were grinning, and laughing, and jeering, and mocking at the sight of tears—weak, womanish, stupid tears—on the face of a strong man.

I was ashamed, but I was yet more angry, and to escape from the danger of an outbreak of my wrath I turned quickly aside, and walked rapidly down a narrow alley.

As I did so a second paper dropped to the ground from the sheet of my wife's letter. Before I had picked it up I saw what it was. It was a message from my boy himself, in the handwriting of his nurse.

"He is brighter to-night," the good creature herself wrote at the top of the page, "and he would insist on dictating this letter."

"My dear, dear papa—"
     When I had read thus far I was conscious again that the yelling, barking, bleating mob behind were looking after me. To avoid the torment of their gaze I hurried on, passed down a second alley, and then turned into a narrow opening which seemed to be the mouth of a third. But I paid small heed to my footsteps, for all my mind was with the paper which I wished to read.

Finding myself in a quiet place at length, I read it. The words were my little darling's own, and I could hear his voice as if he were speaking them:

"My dear, dear papa,
     I am ill with my throat, and sometimes I can't speak. Last night the ceiling was falling down on me, and the fire was coming up to the bed. But I'm werry nearly all right now. We are going to have a Thanksgiving party soon—me, and Jumbo, and Scotty, the puppy. When are you coming home? Do you live in a tent in Morocco? I have a fire in my bedroom: do you? Write and send me some foreign stamps from Tangier. Are the little boys black in Morocco? Nurse showed me a picture of a lady who lives there, and she's all black except her lips, and her mouth stands out. Have you got a black servant? Have you got a horse to ride on? Is he black? I am tired now. Good-night. Mama says I must not tell you to come home quick. Jumbo's all right. He grunts when you shove him along. So good-night, papa. x x x x. These kisses are all for you. I am so thin.
                                        From your little boy,
                                        NOEL."

Come home! Yes, my darling, I will come home. Nothing shall stop me now—nothing, nothing! The sun is almost set. Everything is ready. The men must be saddling the horses again. In less than half an hour I shall have started afresh. I will ride all night to-night and all day to-morrow, and in a week I shall be standing by your side. A week! How long! how long! Lord of life and death, keep my boy alive until then!

I became conscious that I was speaking hot words such as these aloud. Even agony like mine has its lucidities of that kind. At the same moment I heard footsteps somewhere behind me. They were slow and steady footsteps, but I knew them too well. The blood rushed to my head and back to my heart. I looked up and around. Where was I? Where? Where?

I was in a little court, surrounded by low, white-washed walls. Before me there was an inner compartment roofed by a rude dome. From the apex of this dome there floated a tiny white flag. I was in a saint's house. In the confusion of my mind, and the agonizing disarray of all my senses, I had stumbled into the sacred place unawares.

The footsteps came nearer. They seemed to be sounding on the back of my neck. I struggled forward a few paces. By a last mechanical resource of despair I tried to conceal myself in the inner chamber. I was too late. A face appeared in the opening at which I had entered. It was Larby's face, contracted into a grimacing expression.

I read the thought of the man's face as by a flash of light. "Good, Sidi, good! You have done my work as well as my master's. You are a dead man; no one will know, and I need never to lift my hand to you."

At the next instant the face was gone. In the moment following I lived a lifetime. My brain did not think; it lightened. I remembered the death of the American in the streets of Fez. I recalled the jeering crowd at the top of the alley. I reflected that Larby was gone to tell the mob that I had dishonored one of their sanctuaries. I saw myself dragged out, trampled under foot, torn to pieces, and then smuggled away in the dusk on a donkey's back under panniers of filth. My horses ready, my men waiting, my boy dying for want of me, and myself dead in a dunghill.

"Great Jehovah, lend me Thy strength!" I cried, as I rushed out into the alley. Larby was stealing away with rapid steps. I overtook him; I laid hold of him by the hood of his jellab. He turned upon me. All my soul was roused to uncontrollable fury. I took the man in both my arms, I threw him off his feet, I lifted him by one mighty effort high above my shoulders and flung him to the ground.

HALL CAINE

He began to cry out, and I sprang upon him again and laid hold of his throat. I knew where to grip, and not a sound could he utter. We were still in the alley, and I put my left hand into the neck of his kaftan and dragged him back into the saint's house. He drew his dagger and lunged at me. I parried the thrust with my foot and broke his arm with my heel. Then there was a moment of horrible bedazzlement. Red flames flashed before me. My head grew dizzy. The whole universe seemed to reel beneath my feet. The man was doubled backward across my knee. I had drawn my knife—I knew where to strike—and "For my boy, my boy!" I cried in my heart.

It was done. The man died without a groan. His body collapsed in my hands, rolled from my knee, and fell at my feet—doubled up, the head under the neck, the broken arm under the trunk in a heap, a heap.

Oh! oh! Larby! Larby!

Then came an awful revulsion of feeling. For a moment I stood looking down, overwhelmed with the horror of my act. In a sort of drunken stupor I gazed at the wide-open eyes, and the grimacing face fixed in its hideousness by the convulsion of death. O God! O God! what had I done! what had I done!

But I did not cry out. In that awful moment an instinct of self-preservation saved me. The fatal weapon dropped from my hand, and I crept out of the place. My great strength was all gone now. I staggered along, and at every step my limbs grew more numb and stiff.

But in the alley I looked around. I knew no way back to my people except that way by which I came. Down the other alley and through the crowd of idlers I must go. Would they be there still? If so, would they see in my face what I had done?

I was no criminal to mask my crime. In a dull, stupid, drowsy, comatose state I tottered down the alley and through the crowd. They saw me; they recognized me; I knew that they were jeering at me, but I knew no more.

"Skaïrî!" shouted one, and "Shaïrî!" shouted another, and as I staggered away they all shouted "Skaïrî!" together.

Father, they called me a drunkard. I was a drunkard indeed, but I was drunk with blood.

The sun had set by this time. Its last rays were rising off the gilded top of the highest minaret in a golden mist that looked like flame leaping out of a kiln. I saw that, as I saw everything, through a palpitating haze.

When at length I reached the place where I had left my people I found the horses saddled, the mules with their burdens packed on their panniers, the men waiting, and everything ready. Full well I knew that I ought to leap to my seat instantly and be gone without delay; but I seemed to have lost all power of prompt action. I was thinking of what I wanted to do, but I could not do it. The men spoke to me, and I know that I looked vacantly into their faces and did not answer. One said to another, "Sidi is growing deaf."

The other touched his forehead and grinned.

I was fumbling with the stirrup of my saddle when the English Consul came up and hailed me with cheerful spirits. By an effort that was like a spasm I replied.

"Allow me, doctor," he said, and he offered his knee that I might mount.

"Ah, no, no," I stammered, and I scrambled to my seat.

While I was fumbling with my double rein I saw that he was looking at my hand.

"You've cut your fingers, doctor," he said.

There was blood on them. The blood was not mine, but a sort of mechanical cunning came to my relief. I took out my handkerchief and made a pretense to bind it about my hand.

Alee, the guide, was at my right side settling my lumbering foot in my stirrup. I felt him touch the sheath of my knife, and then I remembered that it must be empty.

"Sidi has lost his dagger," he said. "Look!"

The Consul, who had been on my left, wheeled round by the horse's head, glanced at the useless sheath that was stuck in the belt of my jacket, and then looked back into my stupid face.

"Sidi is ill," he said quietly; "ride quickly, my men, lose no time, get him out of the country without delay!"

I heard Alee answer, "Right—all right!"

Then the Consul's servant rode up—he was a Berber—and took his place at the head of our caravan.

"All ready?" asked the Consul, in Arabic.

"Ready," the men answered.

"Then away, as if you were flying for your lives!"

The men put spurs to their mules, Alee gave the lash to my horse, and we started.

"Good-by, doctor," cried the Consul; "may you find your little son better when you reach home!"

I shouted some incoherent answers in a thick, loud voice, and in a few minutes more we were galloping across the plain outside the town.

The next two hours are a blank in my memory. In a kind of drunken stupor I rode on and on. The gray light deepened into the darkness of night, and the stars came out. Still we rode and rode. The moon appeared in the southern sky and rose into the broad whiteness of the stars overhead. Then consciousness came back to me, and with it came the first pangs of remorse. Through the long hours of that night ride one awful sight stood up constantly before my eyes. It was the sight of that dead body, stark and cold, lying within that little sanctuary behind me, white now with the moonlight, and silent with the night.

O Larby, Larby! You shamed me. You drove me from the world. You brought down your mother to the grave. And yet, and yet—must I absolve your murderer?

Father, I reached my home at last. At Gibraltar I telegraphed that I was coming, and at Dover I received a telegram in reply. Four days had intervened between the despatch of my message and the receipt of my wife's. Anything might have happened in that time, and my anxiety was feverish. Stepping on to the Admiralty Pier, I saw a telegraph boy bustling about among the passengers from the packet with a telegram in his hand.

"What name?" I asked.

He gave one that was not my own and yet sounded like it.

I looked at the envelope. Clearly the name was intended for mine. I snatched the telegram out of the boy's hand. It ran: "Welcome home; boy very weak, but not beyond hope."

I think I read the words aloud, amid all the people, so tremendous was my relief, and so overwhelming my joy. The messenger got a gold coin for himself and I leaped into the train.

At Charing Cross I did not wait for my luggage, but gave a foolish tip to a porter and told him to send my things after me. Within half a minute of my arrival I was driving out of the station.

What I suffered during those last moments of waiting before I reached my house no tongue of man could tell. I read my wife's telegram again, and observed for the first time that it was now six hours old. Six hours! They were like six days to my tortured mind.

From the moment when we turned out of Oxford Street until we drew up at my own door in Wimpole Street I did not once draw breath.

And being here I dared hardly lift my eyes to the window lest the blinds should be down.

I had my latch-key with me, and I let myself in without ringing. A moment afterward I was in my darling's room. My beloved wife was with our boy, and he was unconscious. That did not trouble me at all, for I saw at a glance that I was not too late.

Throwing off my coat, I sent to the surgery for my case, dismissed my dear girl with scant embraces, drew my darling's cot up to the window, and tore down the curtains that kept out the light, for the spring day was far spent.

Then, being alone with my darling, I did my work. I had trembled like an aspen leaf until I entered his room, but when the time came my hand was as firm as a rock and my pulse beat like a child's.

I knew I could do it, and I did it. God had spared me to come home, and I had kept my vow. I had traveled ten days and nights to tackle the work, but it was a short task when once begun.

After I had finished I opened the door to call my wife back to the room. The poor soul was crouching with the boy's nurse on the threshold, and they were doing their utmost to choke their sobs.

"There!" I cried, "there's your boy! He'll be all right now."

The mischief was removed, and I had never a doubt of the child's recovery.

My wife flung herself on my breast, and then I realized the price I had paid for so much nervous tension. All the nerves of organic life seemed to collapse in an instant.

"I'm dizzy; lead me to my room," I said.

My wife brought me brandy, but my hand could not lift the tumbler to my mouth, and when my dear girl's arms had raised my own, the glass rattled against my teeth. They put me to bed; I was done—done.

God will forgive him. Why should not I?

Father, that was a month ago, and I am lying here still. It is not neurasthenia of the body that is killing me, but neurasthenia of the soul. No doctor's drug will ever purge me of that. It is here like fire in my brain, and here like ice in my heart. Was my awful act justifiable before God? Was it right in the eyes of Him who has written in the tables of His law, *Thou shalt do no murder*? Was it murder? Was it crime? If I outraged the letter of the holy edict, did I also wrong its spirit?

Speak, speak, for pity's sake, speak. Have mercy upon me, as you hope for mercy. Think where I was and what fate was before me. Would

I do it again in spite of all? Yes, yes, a thousand, thousand times, yes. I will go to God with that word on my lips, and He shall judge me.

And yet I suffer these agonies of doubt. Life was always a sacred thing to me. God gave it, and only God should take it away. He who spilt the blood of his fellow-man took the government of the world out of God's hands. And then—and then—father, have I not told you all?

Yes, yes, the Father of all fathers will pardon him.

On the day when I arrived at Tangier from Fez I had some two hours to wait for the French steamer from Malaga that was to take me to Cadiz. In order to beguile my mind of its impatience, I walked through the town as far as the outer Sôk—the Sôk de Barra.

It was market day, Thursday, and the place was the same animated and varied scene as I had looked upon before. Crushing my way through the throng, I came upon the saint's house near the middle of the market. The sight of the little white structure with its white flag brought back the tragedy I saw enacted there, and the thought of that horror was now made hellish to my conscience by the memory of another tragedy at another saint's house.

I turned quickly aside, and stepping up to the elevated causeway that runs in front of the tents of the brassworkers, I stood awhile and watched the Jewish workmen hammering the designs on their trays.

Presently I became aware of a little girl who was sitting on a bundle of rushes and plaiting them into a chain. She was a tiny thing, six years of age at the utmost, but with the sober look of a matron. Her sweet face was the color of copper, and her quiet eyes were deep blue. A yellow gown of some light fabric covered her body, but her feet were bare. She worked at her plaiting with steady industry, and as often as she stopped to draw a rush from the bundle beneath her she lifted her eyes and looked with a wistful gaze over the feeding-ground of the camels, and down the lane to the bridge, and up by the big house on the hillside to where the sandy road goes off to Fez.

The little demure figure, amid so many romping children, interested and touched me. This was noticed by a Jewish brassworker before whose open booth I stood and he smiled and nodded his head in the direction of the little woman.

"Dear little Sobersides," I said; "does she never play with other children?"

"No," said the Jew, "she sits here every day, and all day long—that is, when her father is away."

"Whose child is she?" I asked. An awful thought had struck me.

"A great rascal's," the Jew answered, "though the little one is such an angel. He keeps a spice shop over yonder, but he is a guide as well as a merchant, and when he is out on a journey the child sits here and waits and watches for his coming home again. She can catch the first sight of travelers from this place and she knows her father at any distance. See!—do you know where she's looking now? Over the road by El Minzah—that's the way from Fez. Her father has gone there with a Christian."

The sweat was bursting from my forehead.

"What's his name?" I asked.

"The Moors call him Larby," said the Jew, "and the Christians nickname him Ananias. They say he is a Spanish renegade, escaped from Ceuta, who witnessed to the Prophet and married a Moorish wife. But he's everything to the little one—bless her innocent face! Look! do you see the tiny brown dish at her side? That's for her drinking water. She brings it full every day, and also a little cake of bread for her dinner.

"She's never tired of waiting, and if Larby does not come home to-night she'll be here in the morning. I do believe that if anything happened to Larby she would wait until doomsday."

My throat was choking me, and I could not speak. The Jew saw my emotion, but he showed no surprise. I stepped up to the little one and stroked her glossy black hair.

"Hoolia?" I said.

She smiled back into my face and answered, "Iyyeh"—yes.

I could say no more; I dare not look into her trustful eyes and think that he whom she waited for would never come again. I stooped and kissed the child, and then fled away.

God show me my duty. The Priest or the Man—which?

Listen! do you hear him? That's the footstep of my boy overhead. My darling! He is well again now. My little sunny laddie! He came into my bedroom this morning with a hop, skip, and a jump—a gleam of sunshine. Poor innocent, thoughtless boy. They will take him into the country soon, and he will romp in the lanes and tear up the flowers in the garden.

My son, my son! He has drained my life away; he has taken all my strength. Do I wish that I had it back? Yes, but only—yes, only that I might give it him again. Hark! That's his voice, that's his laughter. How happy he is! When I think how soon—how very soon—when I think that I—

God sees all. He is looking down on little Hoolia waiting, waiting, waiting where the camels come over the hills, and on my little Noel laughing and prancing in the room above us.

Father, I have told you all at last. There are tears in your eyes, father. You are crying. Tell me, then, what hope is left? You know my sin, and you know my suffering. Did I do wrong? Did I do right?

My son, God's law was made for man, not man for His law. If the spirit has been broken where the letter has been kept, the spirit may be kept where the letter has been broken. Your earthly father dare not judge you. To your Heavenly Father he must leave both the deed and the circumstance. It is for Him to justify or forgive. If you are innocent, He will place your hand in the hand of him who slew the Egyptian and yet looked on the burning bush. And if you are guilty, He will not shut His ears to the cry of your despair.

He has gone. I could not tell him. It would have embittered his parting hour; it would have poisoned the wine of the sacrament. O, Larby! Larby! flesh of my flesh, my sorrow, my shame, my prodigal—my son.

A Note About the Author

Hall Caine (1853–1931) was a British author whose novels, short stories, poems, and criticism made him the most successful writer of his day. Born in Liverpool, Caine trained as an architectural draftsman before becoming a successful lecturer and theater critic. He then moved to London to live and work with the famous Pre-Raphaelite artist Dante Gabriel Rossetti, at which point Caine's literary career began in earnest. He went on to publish dozens of novels, stories, and plays, some of which would inspire important films from directors such as Alfred Hitchcock. Toward the end of Caine's career, he involved himself in local and international politics, undertaking humanitarian trips to Russia and advocating for American support for Allied forces during the Great War.

A Note from the Publisher

Spanning many genres, from non-fiction essays to literature classics to children's books and lyric poetry, Mint Edition books showcase the master works of our time in a modern new package. The text is freshly typeset, is clean and easy to read, and features a new note about the author in each volume. Many books also include exclusive new introductory material. Every book boasts a striking new cover, which makes it as appropriate for collecting as it is for gift giving. Mint Edition books are only printed when a reader orders them, so natural resources are not wasted. We're proud that our books are never manufactured in excess and exist only in the exact quantity they need to be read and enjoyed.

Discover more of your favorite classics with Bookfinity™.

- Track your reading with custom book lists.
- Get great book recommendations for your personalized Reader Type.
- Add reviews for your favorite books.
- AND MUCH MORE!

Visit **bookfinity.com** and take the fun Reader Type quiz to get started.

Enjoy our classic and modern companion pairings!